The Critics Hail . . .

THE FIERCE DISPUTE
"Lyrical, highly descriptive . . . Poignant."
—*Nashville Tennessean*

"As timely today as it was back in 1929."
—*Indianapolis Star*

"The same delicacy and finely tuned sense of detail that lent *Ladies . . .* its principal charm."
—*Cleveland Plain Dealer*

"Timeless . . . genteel and tasteful!"
—*Milwaukee Journal*

HERBS AND APPLES
"A sure touch that charms . . . Leisurely, lyrical."
—*Publishers Weekly*

". . . AND LADIES OF THE CLUB"
"Re-creates an American period . . . with a combination of delicacy and candor."
—*The New York Times*

"A great novel . . . American to its core."
—New York *Daily News*

BAKOS PAPERBACK EXCHANGE
56335 29 PALMS HWY
YUCCA VALLEY, CA 92284

ALSO BY HELEN HOOVEN SANTMYER

NOVELS:

"... And Ladies of the Club"

Herbs and Apples

NONFICTION:

Ohio Town

HELEN HOOVEN SANTMYER

THE FIERCE DISPUTE

ST. MARTIN'S PRESS / NEW YORK

St. Martin's Press titles are available at quantity discounts for sales promotions, premiums or fund raising. Special books or book excerpts can also be created to fit specific needs. For information write to special sales manager, St. Martin's Press, 175 Fifth Avenue, New York, N.Y. 10010.

Grateful acknowledgment is made for permission to reprint the profile of Helen Hooven Santmyer, which appeared in somewhat different form as "Helen Santmyer and Her Ladies of the Club" in *The Magazine, Dayton Daily News,* July 1, 1984. Copyright © 1984 by Roz Young.

The Fierce Dispute was originally published by Houghton Mifflin Co.

THE FIERCE DISPUTE

Copyright © 1987 by the Estate of Helen Hooven Santmyer.

Foreword copyright © 1987 by Weldon A. Kefauver. The three poems, "Before I Go to Sleep," "To the Egyptian Lady in the Boston Museum," and "The Dark House" copyright © 1987 by the Estate of Helen Hooven Santmyer.

All rights reserved. No part of this book may be used or reproduced in any manner whatsoever without written permission except in the case of brief quotations embodied in critical articles or reviews. For information address St. Martin's Press, 175 Fifth Avenue, New York, N.Y. 10010.

Library of Congress Catalog Card Number: 87-16265

ISBN: 0-312-91028-2   Can. ISBN: 0-312-91029-0

Printed in the United States of America

St. Martin's hardcover edition published 1987
First St. Martin's Press mass market edition/October 1988

10 9 8 7 6 5 4 3 2 1

PUBLISHER'S NOTE

Weldon A. Kefauver, the editor who first read and recommended the publication of Helen Hooven Santmyer's famous third novel, ". . . And Ladies of the Club," has been called her literary rediscoverer, and the publisher is grateful to him for contributing the following pages of introduction.

The Fierce Dispute is the second of two early published novels by Helen Hooven Santmyer. Her first, *Herbs and Apples,* was published in 1925 by Houghton Mifflin, and *The Fierce Dispute* followed four years later from that same Boston publisher. Both novels were unavailable for almost sixty years, and would probably never have resurfaced were it not for the chain of events begun with the arrival on Mr. Kefauver's desk of the manuscript of her only nonfiction work, *Ohio Town,* in 1961.

"I realized with the very first paragraph that I had

something extraordinary in my hands." The manuscript had come to Mr. Kefauver via a friend of Ms. Santmyer's, the historian Walter Rumsey Marvin, who was then executive director of the Ohioana Library Association. *Ohio Town* was published the next year by Mr. Kefauver at the Ohio State University Press. But his first opportunity to meet the author came at a post-publication cocktail party given for her by one of her former roommates at Wellesley College.

"She was very much unlike what I expected," he recalls. "She wore a Garboesque red felt hat and smoked unfiltered Camels. The butler, who asked her what she would like to drink, was told she would like some straight bourbon. So she was more than just the genteel lady writer from Xenia that the folklore would have her be at that time."

Ohio Town won a number of local and regional honors, and Mr. Kefauver corresponded with Helen Hooven Santmyer for almost two decades thereafter, mostly about the long novel on which he knew her to be working. It was called " . . . *And Ladies of the Club,*" and when it was finished, she sent it to him.

"Here again I realized, not very far into it, that it was a remarkable thing. I had been somewhat skeptical about the likelihood of our university press taking on a work of fiction, even though Louisiana State University Press had recently published John Kennedy Toole's novel, *A Confederacy of Dunces,* which won a Pulitzer Prize. But I read the entire manuscript—all eight or ten boxes of it—and I recommended it to the editorial board. Happily, and somewhat to my surprise, the board endorsed its publication."

When " . . . *And Ladies of the Club*" was republished two years later by G.P. Putnam's Sons in New York City, it became a national bestseller and Book-of-the-Month Club main selection.

Soon after the 1962 publication of *Ohio Town,* curiosity had drawn Weldon A. Kefauver to a library where he located a copy of the 1929 edition of *The Fierce Dispute,* a novel that Helen Hooven Santmyer had spoken of almost dismissively. "I liked *The Fierce Dispute* very much," he recalls. "It is the first novel she set in Xenia, Ohio—the town that became the locale of all her subsequent books. *The Fierce Dispute* has a very special quality, and it introduces many of the themes that she was to treat at the end of her career. Her statement of these themes in this early novel is perhaps even clearer than it was later."

As her longtime friend and mentor, Mr. Kefauver had always felt certain that one day Helen Hooven Santmyer's fiction would find a wide new readership. "I'm pleased that it happened in her lifetime. My only regret is that this recognition did not come sooner."

Helen Hooven Santmyer died in 1986, at the age of ninety. Her first novel, *Herbs and Apples,* is also available in paperback from St. Martin's Press.

FOREWORD

I WAS NOT, IN THE EARLY 1960s AS THE THEN MANAGING EDITOR OF THE OHIO STATE UNIVERSITY PRESS, THE SEASONED SCHOLARLY publisher I may have more nearly resembled when, during the last two decades of my tenure at the press, I served as its director; but I had, even at that early stage, learned the hard but not necessarily bitter lesson of my chosen profession: that the *succès d'estime* is more often than not the principal—or even the only—reward that practitioners of the art and science of scholarly publishing can look forward to. For our careers are largely spent in service to often extremely small communities of scholars, who rely upon us to make public (no matter how narrowly that public is defined) whatever new knowledge is brought to light that will assist them in their continuing struggle, as specialists, to learn more and more about less and less. In my youthful and hence wilder imaginings, however, I harbored the hope—not, by any means, out of resentment or even discontent—that I might someday be privileged to publish for a much larger—perhaps even a popular or mass—audience.

I thought that that day might, indeed, be imminent when, on some now forgotten date early in the decade, I received the manuscript of Helen Hooven Santmyer's *Ohio Town,* the autobiographical work in which she reflected on her own life, and those of her family, neighbors, and friends, in the town of Xenia, Ohio, during the first half of the present century. Indeed, by the time I had finished the first page of the manuscript's opening chapter, I was all but persuaded that I had detected in Miss Santmyer's writing that universality that is customarily invoked only when we attempt to explain the enduring appeal of the world's greatest authors. For it seemed to me then (and I remain convinced of it now) that the very essence of Santmyer's art is that uncanny ability by which our best writers manage, through skilled manipulation of their texts, to transport us imperceptibly from the mundane, the ordinary, and the prosaic to a metaphoric and poetic level at which what is familiar in our lives becomes the stuff of a larger and more durable reality in which all of us participate and by which we are both defined and exalted.

My experience was much the same when, two decades following publication of *Ohio Town,* I first looked into the formidably bulky manuscript of "*. . . And Ladies of the Club,*" the novel on which, Miss Santmyer had reported to me at various times in the intervening years, she had been almost constantly at work. In her fiction, one finds again— freshly, and as if for the first time—that same carefully modulated voice, pitched exactly to entice and refresh a vagrant sensibility dulled by the shrill insistence of other modern writers that our attention *will* be riveted, and speaking in stately and measured periods of the lives of men, women, and children who are as easily recognized and familiar as ourselves. And here, too, in this chronicle of lives that span generations, that are often quiet but seldom desperate, and that are spent in one, strategically circumscribed locale (which is conspicuously bereft of those "fair streets and singing towers and classic arcades" for which the young Helen Santmyer at one time yearned), there occur those subtle shifts by which one is lifted out of the quotidian and the commonplace to where, it suddenly becomes plain to us, we have always if unknowingly been, to arrive at a consciousness elevated beyond change and independent of time, which is, we are all at once made aware, the true *mise en scène* in which are played out the dramas of our vexed and recalcitrant humanity.

Following the "media event" (the *succès fou,* if you will) that the republication of *". . . And Ladies of the Club"* under commercial auspices occasioned, and the subsequent successes of reprints of both *Ohio Town* and Miss Santmyer's first novel, *Herbs and Apples,* I was often asked by publicists, critics, and readers alike questions prompted by their curiosity about what, exactly, had been the author's intention and purpose in writing the books that, so late in her life, had brought her the fame that she herself could only describe as "astonishing." It was assumed, I gather, by those who made these inquiries of me that, as the original publisher of two of the books on which so much attention had been but lately lavished, and as one who had, after all, over twenty or more years, enjoyed a friendship and conducted a correspondence with Miss Santmyer, I was, perhaps, one step closer to the wellspring of her inspiration, and in possession of some magic key with which to unlock the mystery of what she was about during those long years of isolated scribbling in an obscure midwestern town far removed from the literary capitals of the world. I had no such skeleton key, of course, but I had, certainly, discussed with Helen, both in meetings with her and in letters, what were her expectations of her readers and what she wanted them to gain from her books.

And so I undertook to compose a paragraph of pithy substance, in which I set down in a few sentences of artful construction, what I took to be the nature of the Santmyer literary enterprise. The result, it struck me, was coherent, balanced, sensible, and, above all, instructive—if not actually definitive; and I sent it off to Helen in Xenia, confident that she would give it enthusiastic and not merely pro forma approval. What I received back from her, however, was my precious draft, emended with but one incontrovertible sentence: "No, this is not at all what I had in mind." And though I might have wished I had been put down with a riposte as apposite (and quotable) as Samuel Beckett's famous comment that Joyce's *Finnegans Wake* is "not *about* something; it is that something itself," I was eventually reconciled to the fact that I had gotten precisely what I deserved.

Still, the question nags, as it invariably must when we confront a writer who is serious and whose mastery of the craft of fiction and its closely related genre, autobiography, compels us to take seriously that she *is* serious. And though I continue to think that I do understand—for my own purposes, at any rate—what is the something about which Helen Santmyer wrote (and we can all find support for our private musings on any work of literary art in Professor Eliseo Vivas's reminder that, with the invention of the human unconscious, no author could ever again be sure that he knew for a fact the sources of his inspiration), I shall never again presume to speak for an author who has bequeathed to us the remarkable "something" of her splendid books.

I violate, however, no trust Helen may ever have placed in me, when I attempt to analyze what, in large part, constitutes her appeal for readers like myself. And that is, I think, quite simply, that she constructs for us a universe that is somehow commensurate with the dimensions of the potential of the human spirit. And this is indeed a rarity in an age in which literature commonly represents us to ourselves as isolates and enigmas in a physical and moral universe no longer matched to our intellectual capacities—an impenetrable mystery made no more comprehensible by the workings of our mental processes than it is observable by our senses.

We are, for better or worse, heirs of the naturalists in literature, and contemporaries of those latter-day shapers of the modern sensibility, the existentialists, absurdists, and others who, with their imitators (those who lack the integrity and conviction of the models they exploit, but facilely appropriate their manner, in order to produce meretricious fiction of the kind often dramatized on television), posit a universe that, in a fairly wide variety of versions and permutations, is deprived of the possibility of any benign intervention on the part of a now discredited providence, and is, therefore, without purpose and without soul—alien, inhospitable, indifferent, and perhaps even inimical to man. It is the moral equivalent of the physical universe that many scientists would have us dimly envision as expanding outward at an incredible speed and to no apparent end from the center of a primeval explosion, the detritus of which is, in minuscule part, our home, suspended in an infinity that is beyond human imagining, but is, we are told, shaped like an inverted saddle.

The universe of the Santmyer *oeuvre* is of a very different order. I believe that Helen was never much interested in the abstractions that, throughout the years in which she wrote, were said, in the academic centers of literary scholarship and criticism and in the columns of popular literary pundits, to have shaped serious writing in her time (though there is some evidence that she was determined, at one point, to refute them in her fiction). She preferred to concentrate her energies on the manageable world, on making coherent and intelligible the lives of the characters with whom she was preoccupied, those whom she could observe closely in the complexity of their interactions, free of any notion that only the imposition of imponderable forces from without (or from within) could possibly explain and justify their behavior in the problematic condition in which they find themselves.

The scale of Santmyer's universe is a human scale. The characters in her novels act in circumstances that, though not always congenial, do not abrogate the sense and significance of action. If, as some aestheticians maintain, the highest expression of which man is capable is realized in his ability to fashion a symbol for himself (a statue, a painting, a character in a play or novel) and then to place that symbol in a symbol of the universe that is also his construction (a temple, a shrine, a gallery, or a theater), and to make his fellow beings sensible of what he has done, then it is the achievement of Helen Santmyer that the men and women whose lives she traces in such scrupulous detail, and with an eye as steady and unrelenting as it is compassionate, are securely placed in their cosmos and in hers. And so it is that we, her readers, discover ourselves in her fiction as actors in a universe that, if it is not tailored precisely to the measure of our needs and aspirations, our hopes and expectations, does not, at least, demean our intelligence, but is, like that bright blue marble in space described by the returning Apollo astronauts as the home planet where men can breathe and feed and love and procreate and die, the place where man belongs—or where, at any rate, he finds himself.

To those of us who first entered the world of Helen Hooven Santmyer in the pages of *Ohio Town,* then went on to examine more of the panorama that, like a pointillist painter, she constructed with a myriad of meticulous and deft small strokes in *". . . And Ladies of the Club"* and *Herbs and Apples,* the first novel that preceded it by half a century, the republication of the present edition of her second novel, *The Fierce Dispute,* is a literary event of signal importance. We turn to it, in eager anticipation of being once more invigorated by the spectacle of men and women who, though much exercised, satisfy us that they are not misplaced in the only universe and world they will ever inhabit. As players in the drama "of birth, of childhood, of growing up and falling in love—of growing old and dying," they are privileged to suffer and survive "all the hard, sometimes bitter but always rewarding experience of being men and women."

—WELDON A. KEFAUVER
Columbus, Ohio
July 12, 1987

THE
FIERCE
DISPUTE

Before I Go to Sleep

I have some things to think about before I go to sleep:
The violets along the edges of the stream,
The cattails in the sedges and the gleam
Of a red-winged blackbird's color in his flying swing and
    sweep.

Of the way the May wind sent the maple seeds a-going,
And shook the petals from the cherry trees;
A sudden puff would come, and then the breeze
Would shake the dandelions and set their gray heads
    blowing.

I picked a dandelion and blew it once, twice, thrice,
All the seeds set free and flying far away,
"Mother wanted me," that is the sign, they say.
She was baking in the kitchen, and it smelled so nice!

I ran in and I told her that the dandelion sent me,
And she laughed and said, "Of course I want you child—
To kiss you," and she did, and we both smiled:
And I was glad I minded when the dandelion sent me.

Today has been the nicest day, and now I lie in bed
And think of that May-wind and of the things my Mother
    said.

To the Egyptian Lady in the Boston Museum

With that same smile, scornful and sad and tender
You thought of love, and of those summer days
Gone in a night of many thousand years.
You sat in heavy-scented golden splendor,
The courtly throng, the pomp and power and praise
Lost to unseeing eyes, unheeding ears.
    —Only the artist caught your wandering gaze.

He did not understand the scorn and sadness,
But carved your smile in this enduring guise
A dwelling for your spirit in the tomb.
You knew that love is but a fleeting madness,
That each man lives alone and lonely dies—
You scorned yourself for quailing from your doom,
      Yet thought of love, and met the sculptor's eyes.

And so you smiled, while dynasts came and went,
And sand slipped through your crumbling broken wall,
While silence fell at last on echoing thunder
Of wars that power of ancient empires spent.
While at last, in this bright windy hall,
We pause, who know that love is brief, and wonder,
      If Beauty always is Truth, after all.

The Dark House

I have gone many times past the dark house
And watched for a light
But never has so much as a candle
Broken the night.

I have stood many times by the dark house
And prayed for a sign
But never has a voice from within
Answered mine.

I have gone many times past the dark house
In sorrow and fear.
Would they be so silent who have entered
If they could hear?

Though nothing else await me in the dark house
The night I go up the stair
I shall learn if it is empty
Or if they are there.

1

THE OLD HOUSE FORGOTTEN BY THE TOWNSPEOPLE, STOOD BEHIND PAD-LOCKED GATES AND IRON FENCES, BURIED in a wilderness of maple trees, and lost in encircling acres of knee-deep, billowing grass. Once, for its immensity, its magnificence, it had been the pride of the town. Strangers had been taken out the North Road and shown the opulent villa, with its balconies, bay windows, and towers. A wide drive-way swept across the lawn, around the edge of a terrace and under a *porte-cochère* on the west side of the house. On the south, a straight brick path, bordered by rows of maple trees, led from a side gate to the terrace steps. At that time, the gates had been always open, the driveway crested evenly with gravel, the long brick path meticulously weeded. Brothers and sisters, and brothers- and sisters-in-law, cousins, aunts and uncles had come and gone, day-long, had driven under the *porte-cochère* with a flourish; there had been picnics beneath the trees in summer, and, in winter, balls in the great drawing rooms.

The house had been built, a few years before the war, by the son of one of the large and prosperous pioneer families of southern Ohio. Once upon a time the Linleys had owned most of the township north of the little country town, but those farms had become "Baird land," and the house was "the old Baird place," because Thomas Linley's only daughter Margaret had married John Baird. Now, when only the child Lucy Anne and her mother and her grandmother, that same Margaret Baird, lived there alone—when the gates were closed, and it was only once in a long, long while that any one used the moss-grown path—the townspeople were hardly conscious of the place: they accepted it as they accepted the abandoned gravel pit to the south of town, and the stagnant canal alongside the railroad tracks; it had been absorbed into the landscape.

Children, awed by the solitude, the silence, and the strangeness, sometimes peered curiously through the iron gates. There was little that they could see. The maple branches were so wide flung, so drooping, and so luxuriantly leaved, that they formed an impenetrable screen, and the vista made by the moss-grown path between its two rows of trees came to an end at the terrace steps. Around the house, the grass was clipped short, but everywhere else was left to grow as it would until the season when it could be cut for hay. This paradise of grass so tangled that one could crawl through it unseen, of maple trees that made tents for hiding in, roofed by boughs, walled by grass so tall that it was brushed by the endmost leaves, was a temptation to children—a temptation only enhanced by a suggestion in the air of the mysterious, the unhappy, an aura of desertion, decay. The bolder among them carried across the high fence their games of hide-and-seek, but they did not venture within hailing distance of the house; they caught only fragmentary glimpses through the trees of brick walls, of cold, dead chimneys, or the transient glimmering of sunshine reflected from a black window. The sight of Lucy Anne, playing on the terrace, was enough to send them helter-skelter back across the fence. Not that they feared the child, whose name they did not even know, but where she was, the hired man was apt to be also, and him they did fear. He was an ancient, gnarled, rheumatic negro, who screamed hot and vivid threats and furious abuse at any one caught trampling the uncut hay.

These trespassers lived, most of them, in the tight row of mediocre new houses across the street from the Baird place. This was the last street in the town, which could spread no further in that direction while old Mrs. Baird lived and refused to sell part or parcel of her land. Along the north side of the street, throughout its length, stretched that high iron fence, with its padlocked gates. Outside the fence there was a public sidewalk, but it was overgrown in the summer with knot-grass and Queen Anne's lace, and grasshoppers and crickets lay all day long on the cement in the sun, or hopped chirring into the dusty weeds when disturbed by a rare footfall. Except for the children, none passed there—except for the children and two others.

One of these was Attorney John Robinson, the elderly lawyer who had charge of Mrs. Baird's affairs. He alone, of all the town, could have answered with definite information the conjectures occasionally voiced in the drugstore of an evening. She was not "land-poor," John Baird had not "made away" with the Linley money—the Linley money had never been put into his hands. His widow had not shut herself up, with her daughter and granddaughter, because she was ashamed of her poverty. John Robinson knew that her father's money was safely invested, and that, year after year, she added income to capital. And yet, if any one expressed the suspicion that she might be a miser, he felt inclined to demur; in some ways, certainly, she behaved like one, but she had none of the miser's unamiable traits of character. Nor was she mad, as some surmised; one could hardly call her more than mildly eccentric. Nor did he think the shame of her daughter's disastrous marriage had driven her into seclusion. That might have had something to do with it, but it seemed to him, rather, that she was moved by some inscrutable purpose, some plan for the future. It was not so inscrutable, either, when considered in the light of her will. That preposterous will! It troubled his conscience, it drove him to the very gate of the Baird place, in a determination to remonstrate with her. But the gate was always locked. He lost his courage, invariably, and turned away, promising himself that the next time she came to his office, he would have it out with her. But she was a determined and obstinate old lady, who refused to allow him to open the subject. Persistence would only have driven her to another lawyer, and so his remonstrance took the form of imaginary dialogues with her, carried on in his mind as he walked past the villa, while he remembered with sorrow the grace and beauty of her daughter Hilary, whose life had come now to such cruel waste.

It was the thought of Hilary—and of Hilary alone, as he knew nothing of her mother—that brought young Dr. Martin Child, too, to the gates of the Baird place. His dull boyhood in the vulgar little town had given him but one glamorous memory: only one, but it seemed to him still to have redeemed all the rest. Once upon a time, on every bright sunshiny summer afternoon, Hilary Baird on her spotted pony had cantered down Main Street beneath the elms of the Court House Square, and he had swung on the hitching chains along the curb to watch while she passed. There had been magic in those brief glimpses of her, but he could not think, now, wherein it had lain. She had been, as a child, small for her age, no larger than he, though older. A vivid little thing, black-haired, tanned, hatless, her white skirts in the air, the ends of her brilliant Roman-striped sash streaming on the wind. Cameo-clear was the impression she had made; there were no blurred outlines. She was quick, certain, unhesitant; she alone in a world of stupid, clumsy, blundering people, had known exactly where she was going. So he tried, now, to express the distinction that, as a boy, he could only feel, wordlessly. He had wished, then, that he were older—old as her brother Tom, because if he could have known Tom, then he might have known her. Her other brother, the one who was old enough to be her father, almost, was the one who had brought an end to Hilary's life in the town, for after he had married and his work had taken him abroad, he had sent for her to be with them, to travel, to go to school in Switzerland. Dr. Martin had heard of her marriage, to a musician and a foreigner, while he was at the University; he had tried to picture her as she must have become, and had been forced to struggle against a foolish sense of loss. Now they were both at home again, and again he was wondering about her. With her child she had come away from her husband, and the man had afterwards died. Beyond that, there was no information abroad about her, and he laughed at himself, grown, a physician, respected for his good sense, for still wishing, boyishly, that he might somehow come to know her. His walks availed him nothing. Hilary was never to be seen. The child was sometimes visible, playing on the terrace, and he began to hope that she would carry her games down to the fence, and that he might then be able to make friends with her. With that idea he entertained himself, in his idle moments, and that was why he sometimes strolled the length of the North Road on the "wrong side" of the street.

But the little girl, had he but known it, was not likely to wander so far afield. She had tried it once, and had been grievously abashed.

2

LUCY ANNE HAD LONG BEEN AWARE OF THE CHILDREN WHO CROSSED THE FENCE STEALTHILY WHEN AARON WAS NOT ON guard. She had never summoned him on such occasions. She liked to know that they were there, and pretended that they had come to play with her. And then, one day, she had crept down through the waist-deep grass to the tree where she had seen them hide: she went timidly, planning to ask them to show her their games, as she would show them hers. She would tell them the stories of the place that her grandmother had told her—she would tell them that under the very tree in whose shade they lay, her great-uncle Richard had said good-bye to her great-aunt Sarah before he went off to the war. But when she parted the boughs and looked in upon them where they lay whispering on the bare ground close to the tree trunk, they did not recognize her as a possible friend.

It was fright, perhaps, that they concealed beneath a blustering anger.

"Ol' tattle-tale!" they flung at her. "Go an' tell the ol' hired-man, an' see if we care!"

Bewildered, she saw them back away from her, and vanish down their path of trodden grass. After that, she made no further attempt to gain their acquaintance. She could, perhaps, have understood their feeling that the old house where she lived was awe-inspiring and mysterious, but it would never have occurred to her that in their eyes she partook of that mystery and that awe. She only knew that they would not play with her.

As for the house, when for any reason she had to pass through the endless succession of rooms that were never used, she was chilled to the bone, and she scuttled through the shadows like a small white rabbit, watching, over her shoulder. The paneled hall, the wide uncarpeted staircase, where her footfall left faint ghostly tracks in the dust, where the wood squeaked, and mice chittered behind the panels—the hall was bad enough, even although there was some light there, falling dimly through the narrow dusty bits of glass on either side of the bolted front door. But in the drawing rooms, the inside shutters were closed tight over all the windows, and she could only see to find her way around because all the furniture was shrouded in white covers. Even the chandeliers were tied up in white bags. There were mirrors, one over each mantel, and one between the front windows; they were filmed with dust, but if they caught her eye as she passed, she seemed to see shapes behind her moving as she watched. Only the great square piano in the front drawing room remained uncovered. Perhaps it was too large to cover, or perhaps Lucy Anne's grandmother did not care if it was spoiled by the dust. But that could hardly be it, because Lucy Anne was forbidden even so much as to touch it, with the tip of her little finger. It was a deep, dark color, and the vaguest ray of light came back gleaming from its lucent surface. There was no wood like it in the back part of the house. Rosewood, her grandmother said it was—a rosewood piano.

The other part of the house, where they lived, was not in the least ghostly nor terrifying. The side door at the end of the brick path beneath the straight row of maple trees opened on to a hall that crossed through the house from side to side, and all that lay behind it was warm, friendly, and familiar. First, there was the library, with its tall bookcases whose glass doors squeaked when they were opened, the shabby couch against the wall, the square table, covered with green felt, in the middle of the room, and the stiff rocking chairs that were drawn to the fender on winter evenings. There was one deep leather armchair so worn that the horsehair stuffing came through the cracks, that her mother always sat in with her books or her sewing. Beside the library was her grandmother's bedroom, and behind it the dining room. A bright red mahogany table and a wide mahogany sideboard, with Thomas Linley's heavy ornate silver displayed on it would have made the room the brightest in the house if the morning sun had not been shut out by the heavy green outside shutters. A narrow passage led to the kitchen, a door in the passage wall opened on to the square porch that lay between it and the dining room. Behind the kitchen the house went on for ever and ever: first the summer kitchen, with its rusty old stove, and the well with a green pump that squeaked and rattled and discharged its water explosively just when you had almost given up in exhaustion; then the laundry, where there was another stove, covered with flatirons and copper boilers; then the woodshed and the empty stables. Lucy Anne loved this part of the house. It was rough and black and splintery inside, unpainted and leaky, it smelled pleasantly of rotting timber and of green wood newly cut, of sawdust and shavings, of rain water, steam, starch, and soapsuds. The windows would not open, and outside they were overgrown with trumpet vines. When the red trumpet flowers dropped from the vines, Lucy Anne wore them on her fingers like long stiff gloves, or set them up in rows on the tool-shed bench. Her grandmother had taught her games to play with the flowers, had shown her how to curl the stems of dandelions, how to make ladies of hollyhocks and gentlemen of the ends of spruce branches, and torches, dim and flickering, of onion tops filled with captive fireflies.

These games would have been merry enough had there been anyone to join her in them, but somehow it was not quite satisfactory, pretending that there were Margarets and Elizabeths with her, when she knew that at that very moment, perhaps, there were real little girls, with tight plaits and gingham dresses and grimy hands, hidden under the trees in her own yard, who would only call her names and run from her, if she ventured to appear before them. But Lucy Anne accepted life as she found it, and was in general contented enough.

Out of doors, she had for her only companion Aaron, the hired man. She followed him about his work in the tool shed, in the vegetable gardens, when he was chopping wood, when he was planting a few flower seeds against the foundation of the house, or under the edge of the kitchen porch. (But her grandmother would not let her go with him to the tenant's house on the nearest farm when he went for milk and eggs. It was "too long a walk for a little girl.") Aaron, a taciturn, sullen old negro, had always tolerated her presence, but he had never been really friendly until after the morning when she had followed him to the grindstone and had found him singing beneath his breath "Go down, Moses," as the stone whirled about, and the knife in his hand was ground to a gleaming edge in a swift crescendo whir. When he had slowly straightened his bent back, and looked up, dizzily, he found her staring at him, entranced.

"Sing it again, Aaron, will you, please?"

Flattered, he sang it again. When he had finished, "Aaron, could you teach me to sing it?"

He reckoned, cautiously, that maybe he could.

"Somewhere where Grandmother couldn't hear," she had continued, somewhat to his consternation. Then she explained. "You see, Aaron, she's always telling me I can't sing, and do for goodness' sake stop aggravating her by making that noise. And I should so like to surprise her by showing her that I can sing. So will you, please, Aaron? In the stable would be a good place, I should think."

After that, whenever they could steal away unobserved for an hour in the morning, they would meet in the stable. Aaron would sit on the edge of an empty wheelbarrow, one twisted hand hanging between his knees, the other beating out the rhythm in the air, while he hummed the tune. Lucy Anne would stand before him, swaying a little as she sang, her head thrown back, her small chest heaving.

But these hours were few, on the whole, because her grandmother liked to have Lucy Anne within reach of her eye and voice. Most mornings she played with her dolls on the terrace or on the porch, or up and down the length of the laundry and the tool shed on stormy days in summer when rain drummed lightly on the roof, when the water gurgled in all the spouts and emptied itself in a roaring flood at the corner of the porch where the mint and parsley grew. On such days her grandmother allowed her to wash and iron her dolls' clothes—she even paused, now and again, in the manifold activities that kept her bustling back and forth, to lend a hand at the wringing.

Like many old ladies, she bustled unnecessarily; she was breathless and short and stout—more stout in seeming than in reality, because of her stiff petticoats and her two aprons—on top, one all-enveloping, of blue-checked gingham, and under it, a ruffled white one, with a pair of scissors and a tiny, heart-shaped pincushion dangling from the belt by a long tape, and her spectacle case in its pocket. The gingham apron she wore while she was cooking or washing dishes, or working around the house; when she sat down to sew, or to preside at Lucy Anne's lessons, she took it off, and the immaculate white ruffles emerged resplendent.

Lucy Anne did not go to school. Her grandmother taught her to read and do sums and to find places on a map, and helped her to learn by heart chapters out of the Bible. She kept her books in the deep drawers at the bottom of the library bookcases: she had some story books that were her own, and all the old schoolbooks that had been her mother's, her grandmother's, and her great-grandmother's. These she loved most of all: they were the oldest, and had the yellowest leaves, and the queerest print and the funniest pictures, and smelled the most bookish, and they were bound in crumbling

brown leather, dusty to the touch. Inside the cover
they bore her great-grandmother's name, written in
a spluttery little-girl writing, in faded ink: sometimes "Lucy Anne," sometimes "Lucianne." Her
namesake imitated this vagary conscientiously, in
some of her books spelling it one way, in some, the
other.

She found it comfortable to play her games and
to learn her lessons in the presence of her grandmother, where she felt herself safe against loneliness and was untroubled by incomprehensible
longings and strange make-believes. But she never
considered her grandmother perfect, as her mother
was perfect. For one thing, she was too demonstra-
tive: she too often interrupted the task in hand to
kiss her, or to pat her cheek, or smooth her hair.
Lucy Anne tried not to stiffen rebelliously at the
touch of the affectionate hand, she tried to respond.
She would not for anything have hurt her grandmother's feelings, but she wondered sometimes
why things should have been so contrary, so
twisted, why her mother should have been so different.

Her mother was not exactly a comfortable person. She did not wear aprons: she wore bright-colored linen smocks, and sandals on her feet. She was
little and slender, her features small and clear cut,

with a hollow between the line of her cheekbone and the line of her jaw. Her eyes were a cool gray, her hair smooth, soft and dark, and brushed straight back from the widow's peak in the middle of her forehead. She moved in an intense quiet; she was so folded in upon herself, so remote and untouchable that she seemed to Lucy Anne to have finished with everyday things a long, long while ago. Like a lady in a picture, she sat and waited. Her nearest approach to a caress was an occasional half-smile, amused, tolerant. Lucy Anne would not hurt her, either: she concealed her awed adoration, lest it should make her mother unhappy to find herself the recipient of a love that she could not return. She knew perfectly well that her grandmother loved her more—perhaps a million times more—than her mother did; she knew also that she was unfair to her grandmother because she in return loved her mother more. She strove to hide her feelings, and on one point only did she deliberately take issue with her grandmother. She could not submit without protest to hearing her mother made the subject of mockery.

"Your mother is a funny woman," Lucy Anne's grandmother would say to her, shaking her head and sighing dismally. "She's the funniest woman in the world. I can't understand. . . ."

Then the child would stamp her foot and cry, choked with rage, "She *isn't* funny! . . . She *isn't*, she *isn't* . . . there isn't one single funny thing about her!" But around her heart there would be an icy chill that all her vehemence could not melt.

Her grandmother loved to tease them both.

When they all sat on the little porch between the dining room and the kitchen, in the summer evenings, Lucy Anne sat on the bench beside her grandmother, and suffered her hand to be held, while her mother sat alone in another chair. The child would have liked to sit on the edge of the porch beside her mother—perhaps, even, to lean back against her knees, but instead she remained motionless on the bench, her feet not quite touching the floor, her head thrown back so that she could watch the birds appear and disappear in the blue air over the maple trees, her hand passive in her grandmother's on the seat between them, hidden beneath their skirts, lest Lucy Anne's mother should see.

The little porch faced the west, and there was a gap between the trees that enabled one to look far beyond the acres of grass that flowed in long, slow, spreading waves before the summer wind, to a distant low mass of blue on the horizon. Every fine evening, when the supper dishes had been washed and put away, they would go out there to watch the sun set. Above that far-off blue horizon the sky would turn slowly from flame color to a smoky mother-of-pearl, amethyst and old rose, and dusty saffron. Overhead for a little while there would be a depth of sky not blue, but a clear, pale apple green.

Every evening, Lucy Anne's grandmother would say the same thing.

"Could there be a finer sunset than that, anywhere? I always wonder why folks are so set on traveling. Italy, for instance. You're always thinking about Italy—did you ever see a more gorgeous sunset than that in Italy?"

Lucy Anne had never heard her mother mention Italy. Usually she just laughed in reply to the silly question, but once she stirred a little in her chair and spoke impatiently.

"It isn't for sunsets that people go to Italy."

"No? They go for husbands, I suppose?"

There was a sharp, triumphant note in the retort, as if it had been waiting for a long while for a chance to be said. Lucy Anne let go her grandmother's fingers and folded her hands together in her lap.

1

ON A WET SUMMER MORNING, HILARY SAT
IN THE LOW ROCKING CHAIR BESIDE THE
OPEN KITCHEN WINDOW, SHELLING THE
peas for dinner. While her hands were busy in her
lap she listened to the rain as it dripped steadily
from the leaves of the honeysuckle under the window, as it raced in the gutters at the eaves and
gurgled from the spout at the corner of the house.
Now and again she glanced idly across the angle
between the kitchen window and the open laundry
door, where she could see Lucy Anne at her play.
Hilary's mother was in the laundry, ironing, and the

child sat on the doorsill. The rain spattered about her, but it was a warm rain, and fragrant, filling the damp air with scent of grass and leaf and earth. Lucy Anne's hair curled about her cheeks—rain did that to her always—and she looked a comfortable little old-fashioned thing as she sat there in her checked gingham dress and her white ruffled pinafore, with her socks in wrinkles about her bare brown ankles. She rocked a naked doll on her knees. Through the open window, Hilary could hear all that she said to her grandmother:

"Tell me when the doll's clothes are dry enough to iron, will you, please?"

She drew her knees up to her chin, burying the doll in her lap, and rocked slowly back and forth.

"But what shall I do while I wait . . . ?"

"Oh, I like the rain, Gran. There is a song in it—the wind underneath, and the birds on top, and the sound of the water in it all."

"No, it isn't nonsense. . . . Don't you hear the catbird?"

A sleek gray bird, alert and arrogant, moved about in the heart of the syringa bush. Lucy Anne pursed her lips to imitate the involved outpouring of liquid notes. It was not very successful—who could follow the intricacies of a catbird's song? But her grandmother appeared suddenly in the doorway, as Hilary had known that she would, her iron still in her hand.

" . . . outlandish noise! I won't have it, Lucy Anne. You have as much music in you as a jaybird."

"Oh, Gran!"

"Yes. And I'd like to know," with a quick suspicion, "who taught you to whistle?"

"No one. I just found out one day that I could."

"Now, my child—no fibs."

"Honestly and truly, cross my heart and hope to die! But—but—I have learned to sing. From Aaron."

"From *Aaron?* What do you mean?" The wrathful old lady glared at Lucy Anne. The child drew back, hurt and bewildered.

"You were always saying I couldn't sing. I thought if I learned to, I could surprise you. I—I thought you would like it."

"Like it?"

"You said it was all wrong, the way I sang. But if I learned to do it right—and I can. Listen—"

Before her outraged grandmother could reply, she scrambled to her feet, her dark face glowing and confident. Swaying a little from side to side she began to sing, her voice muted, soft, husky, in obvious imitation of Aaron's, but childishly sweet and true.

"Go down, Moses, go down, Moses, to Egypt's Lan',
Tell ol' Pharaoh, tell ol' Pharaoh, let my people
   go—"

Her grandmother leaned over, seized her elbow, gave her a vicious, quick shake. Lucy Anne caught her breath and stared, incredulous.

"Hush that racket! Colored folks' songs, learned from the hired man! I've a good mind to turn you over my knee!"

"But why—why—why?" burst from the child in a frightened wail. "You act like it was wicked!"

"Not wicked. Tiresome and naughty. You're trying to plague me to death." She released her hold on Lucy Anne's elbow, and with a bewildered air began to smooth down the crisp flat waves of her white hair. It was a sure sign of perturbation. Hilary, in the kitchen, smiled slightly, a secret little smile. A silent child waited and watched; the corners of her mouth drooped dismally, her lower lip trembled.

"Perhaps I'd better let Aaron go—"

"*Aaron?* You won't, you won't—oh, how—" Lucy Anne turned, and with her two arms over her head, struck her fists against the door jamb, hard, and, having stumbled against it, she kicked the unoffending naked doll out into the rain. Then, seeing

28

what she had done, made no effort at rescue, but burst into heartbroken sobs.

Hilary laughed, and went on shelling peas. Her mother stood and waited for the passing of the storm. Presently the sobbing ceased, except for an occasional dramatic wail and more frequent and more spontaneous gulp compounded of tears and lack of breath. Her grandmother spoke quietly.

"Now hush that nonsense, and listen to me. Aaron can stay if you will promise me not to do any more singing."

Lucy Anne lifted her tear-stained face, and stood considering.

"No, I couldn't promise that." She shook her head obstinately. "Because I couldn't remember it. Not any more than if I promised not to breathe."

Her grandmother stiffened, drew away, her stubborn old mouth straight and set. Hilary was amazed, but smiled at her amazement. The child was young to have found such a clear statement for the truth. But it was a truth that her grandmother would never admit.

"So that," she exclaimed, "is what all this play-acting has been for. I suppose your mother put you up to saying that?"

"Mother!" Lucy Anne's reply rang clear, speaking her unfeigned astonishment.

"Don't you tell me she doesn't put you up to it. All these—"

"Mother! Oh, no—she doesn't put me up to *anything.* Mother"—and an ancient incredible hurt sounded in the childish voice—"she never says anything more to me than she just has to say. You know, sometimes, I think she doesn't even like me."

The listening Hilary paled slightly. The grandmother laughed contemptuously, a short, hard, triumphant little sound, but she broke it off sharp as she watched the child's sad face.

"Your mother's a queer woman, Lucy Anne. . . . No, no I'm not teasing you now, so don't stamp your foot." Her voice was again affectionate, grandmotherly. Hilary knew that this was a time-worn game between the two. The child's eagerness in her defense might have been a knife in the heart of any one less steadfastly hardened against attack.

"She's queer, but not queer enough not to like you. You see, when you came to live with me, I made her promise that so long as I lived, you should be my little girl."

For a moment there was silence. Lucy Anne shook her head.

"If she promised that, she couldn't have liked me so very much."

"Well, I like you anyway. And you won't promise to try to please me."

"Oh, yes, I will." Then she hesitated, pondered. "I'll promise not to have any more singing lessons from Aaron. And not to listen to him, singing. I think I can promise when I find myself singing, to stop."

Her grandmother smiled, reluctantly. "Very well. That will have to do."

"But *why,* Gran?"

"Because I ask you to do it for me. Isn't that reason enough?" Then she added, more briskly, "Fetch your doll in out of the rain, and then come in and get one of the clean handkerchiefs I've just ironed. Your doll's clothes must be about dry, too. Come along with me. You may use my littlest iron and the sleeveboard."

Later, when old Mrs. Baird, with the freshly ironed sheets and table linen in her arms, passed through the kitchen, Hilary was still there, in the rocker beside the window. She smiled coolly at her mother.

"Not even Lucy Anne herself can convince you that song is as natural to her as the breath of her body."

Again the old lady's mouth set stubbornly.

"You're wasting *your* breath bringing the subject

up. I won't have it, you know." She shook her head as she laid the linen, still smelling of the heat of the iron, across the back of a chair. "One musician in the family is quite enough. Of all the vagabonds—"

"Who's a vagabond?" Lucy Anne appeared suddenly behind her.

A glint of cruelty shone in her grandmother's eyes as she darted a glance at the immobile, indifferent Hilary.

"Musicians," she answered, shortly.

Again Hilary smiled that cool, sardonic smile. "I protest, Mother. There are some gentlemen among them."

"Then why is one musician in a family enough?" Lucy Anne demanded. "I should think—" Then her tone lifted, quickened from consideration to curiosity. "Who was the musician in our family?"

A blank silence followed. Mrs. Baird separated the sheets and pillow cases from the tablecloths, and gave them to Lucy Anne.

"Put these in the chest of drawers in the upstairs hall, will you? The sheets in the bottom drawer, the pillow slips—"

"But Gran, who—?"

"Your father, Lucy Anne, was a musician. Now you know, and I want you *never to speak of it again.*"

She pushed the child toward the door, and she went out, dazed and chastened.

Hilary rose, with the peashells gathered in a newspaper.

"Mother, I do protest." She spoke quietly. "That's no way to keep a promise."

"She had to know, sooner or later, that her father was a musician."

"That, yes. But might you not as well have said, in so many words, that you considered him a vagabond?"

"So I do."

"But you promised—"

"I promised never to mention him, if you would let me bring her up as I pleased, so long as you stayed here, and if you would never mention him either."

"I have kept my word."

"Have you? Then, why—?"

"She told you herself."

"You think then that it can't be prevented?"

"I think that she is her father's daughter." Hilary faced her mother squarely, a slight flush on her cheeks.

"We shall see, then." The two women stared at each other. There might have been a gauntlet on the floor between them.

2

T HAT DAY THEY ATE THEIR NOONDAY
DINNER IN A STRAINED SILENCE, AND
WASHED THE DISHES ALMOST WITHOUT A
word; when the tea-towels had been rinsed and put
on the rack to dry, and the dishpans hung on their
nails beneath the sink, and the fire banked in the
stove, they separated, the old woman and the young
woman and the child, and went each to be alone
with her thoughts.

Hilary went upstairs to her bedroom, locked the
door and crossed the floor to the chest of drawers
in the corner. She hesitated with her fingers around

the glass knobs of the lowest drawer. She had concealed there a worn and shabby violin case, an
empty violin case. But she did not open the drawer
to take it out. There was no need, after all. She
turned away, and drew a rocking chair around from
the window until it faced the bed, and sat down in
it. She had put behind her the world outside, where
the soft rain still was falling, and the catbird singing
in the syringa bush. On the wall over the bed there
hung an old map, discolored with age—a seven-
teenth-century map of Italy. It was, perhaps, inaccu-
rate, but a beautiful piece of work. Clusters of roofs
marked the towns, the seas were painted Delft blue,
and in the corners were figures costumed princi-
pally in scarlet. Hilary sat in the rocking chair, her
hands folded in her lap, and stared at the map. She
heard, without noticing what she heard, the slow
footsteps of her mother as she came up the stairs,
passed her room, and went through the door into
the front part of the house.

Old Mrs. Baird, who had stopped to change from
a fresh gingham apron into a soiled one, and to
search in a box in the desk for certain keys that she
wanted, was now on her way to the attic.

It was not really an attic, the third floor of the
house. The attic lay still higher, under the roof, a
black-dark stretch of empty space lighted scarcely at

all by grimed dormer windows. The third floor was one of large rooms similar to the bedrooms below, but they were rooms where the walls were unpapered, or the paper was hanging in torn strips; they were uncarpeted, and the wide boards had cracks between them, and were some of them loose at the end. They fulfilled all the functions of an attic: they were piled full of discarded or broken pieces of furniture, rolls of old carpet, bundles of chenille curtains wrapped in broken crumbling newspapers. Framed pictures stood with their faces against the walls. There were rows of trunks, antebellum trunks, with barrel-shaped lids, there were cardboard hatboxes, and carpetbags.

Mrs. Baird unlocked the door of one of the rooms and entered and opened the shutters over the window. Her eyes searched the corners; when she saw what she wanted, she held her apron tight about her, and wormed her way between the trunks. On one of them stood an old chip basket full of daguerreotypes, on another a black chest with a brass handle in the center of its lid. It was perhaps two feet long, and but little more than a foot wide and a foot deep. She lifted it easily by the handle, returned with it and the daguerreotypes to the wall, set them down, went back to close the shutters and to lock the door, then put the basket on the box, lifted them both in her arms and carried them down the two long flights of stairs and into her bedroom. There the breathless old lady dusted them, pushed them under her bed, and went to call her grandchild to her afternoon lessons.

Lucy Anne had gone from the kitchen straight through the laundry and through the workshop to the woodshed, where the winter's supply of wood was already piled almost to the rafters. She climbed cautiously over the unsteady thick blocks, and crawled across them to the window. It was not a window, really, but a little square wooden door which swung open over the driveway. When Aaron brought home a load of wood, he stopped the horse outside and tossed the blocks into the shed through the window. Now Lucy Anne unlatched it and threw it open, so that she could look into the rain-washed world: a bough of the cherry tree, a corner of the stable and the flowers of the trumpet vine that grew about the window were framed like a picture. She sat down on a block of wood, crossed her arms on the sill and leaned on them. But she did not see the cherry tree, nor the stable, nor the trumpet flowers. She was searching her mind for certain memories, queer and uncomprehended mysteries which might now be clearer since the morning's storm.

For she knew certainly, now, that it must have been her father they had meant when, one afternoon last spring, she had heard her mother and her grandmother talking about geniuses. She had been picking the lilies of the valley that grew at the edge of the kitchen porch, when they had paused for a moment at the open kitchen window. They had not seen her through the screen of the honeysuckle vines.

"You're a poor spineless creature, Hilary," she had heard her grandmother say. "If you weren't, you would admit that the man was a knave, and forget him."

"A genius, not a knave. Rules weren't made for geniuses."

"Rubbish! You can't deny he broke your heart when he broke the rules."

"Don't be ridiculous, Mother." The tones were easy, contemptuous. "Of course I deny it."

"Oh? Well, I don't suppose you think you broke his heart?"

"Hardly. But I'm sure he thought so, when he went back and found me gone. If he hadn't, he could never have composed—" and she murmured the title, some phrase in a foreign tongue. "Geniuses make the most of what heart they have."

"A song you've never heard, and a child—"

"Never mind that, now, Mother."

They had moved away then from the window. And for one swift passionate instant Lucy Anne had hated her grandmother, because she had feared that she intended to say "and a child *you didn't want.* . . ."

Lucy Anne stirred unhappily on her block of wood. She put from her the words that had not been spoken, and sought further back in her mind, for the memory of that time when she had been quite small. . . .

She knew now why her grandmother had been so queer when her father was dying. She had not been hidden anywhere that morning when the telegram came; there had been no necessity for concealment, for they had completely forgotten her.

A male creature in uniform, knock-kneed and pimply, had been intercepted on the path by Aaron and brought to the kitchen door. He had a yellow envelope for her mother; he peered curiously into the kitchen while he fumbled in his pocket for a pencil, and while her mother wrote her name on a yellow square of paper: when she gave him back the paper and pencil, he turned reluctantly and went away. Then her mother opened the envelope and spread out another yellow square of paper on the kitchen table.

After she had stared at it for a long while she said, in a small breathless voice, "He's dying. In Chicago."

"And wants you now, I suppose?" Grandmother's tone was cold and sneering. When her mother turned to face her, Lucy Anne stepped to the table and read the paper. It said:

"Mercy hospital Chicago dying peritonitis please come dear Hilary.

"PAOLO"

"Yes," her mother was saying, "he wants me."

"Well, you're not going. Not on my money."

"Mother! He's *dying!*" Lucy Anne could see the heartbeats in the little hollow at the base of her mother's throat. There was something awful in the low cry from the white lips. Lucy Anne was terrified.

"He'll have to die, then, without you, if you can't pay your own railroad fare."

"You know I sold everything I owned to get back here, when—"

"When you'd had enough of him. You came back of your own accord, and now you can just stay here."

All the rest of the day Lucy Anne's mother had

been like a stone, without life, without thought. She had moved in a dreadful stillness, and had not answered to her name.

They were having breakfast in the kitchen again the next morning when the knock-kneed boy came back, with another yellow envelope.

Lucy Anne's father was dead.

Hilary gave the yellow paper to her mother to read.

"It's just as well you didn't start," the old lady said, bluntly. "You couldn't have got there in time."

"As if that mattered."

"You're crazy, Hilary. Why not? He couldn't even have known that you weren't coming."

"But I knew—that I failed him—when he was *dying*. We'll never forget that, Mother, I promise you."

But Lucy Anne thought that they must have forgotten it by this time, because it had never been mentioned again.

It was strange, the difference it had made to her mother—Paolo's being dead. She had always seemed to Lucy Anne to be waiting for someone. Everything she had done had been done with the air of one who, absent-mindedly, fills in an endless stretch of time. Afterwards, she still waited, but not for a person—for something to happen. Lucy Anne knew that there were two ways of waiting. If your grandmother had gone away for the day, as she did, once in a long while, you kept looking out of the window, when it was about time for her, and tried to think of things to do until it wouldn't be silly to look out of the window again, then you hurried with what you had found to do, in case she should come before you had finished. That was the way her mother had behaved once, although she hadn't actually looked out of the window. But if you were waiting for something to happen—a thunder storm—you didn't try to do anything to fill up the time. You gave yourself up to waiting; you knew there was no use thinking of anything else until it was over. That was how her mother waited, now. Lucy Anne, herself, wondered if anything ever would happen, really. She could see that her mother was growing very tired; she spent hours, every day, on the library couch, with her eyes closed, or lay back in her deep leather chair, staring at a book whose pages were never turned. She was growing impatient, too; sometimes there was a hot flush on her cheekbones, a glitter in her eye; she even spoke impatiently, now and then.

Lucy Anne was awakened from her brooding over these things. Her grandmother had called her.

She sighed mournfully, and climbed down from the woodpile. It was lesson time. But this was the history afternoon, and history was not quite so dull as arithmetic or spelling.

The history lessons given Lucy Anne in the afternoons when she sat with her grandmother at the green-felt-covered library table, had always consisted largely of anecdotes about the Bairds, the Linleys, and the Hewitts. Thomas Linley's father had owned a mill in the wilderness of southern Ohio in the early days of the nineteenth century, and Thomas's daughter remembered his stories of backwoodsmen, pioneer settlers, and Indian raids, of the War of 1812, when his father had gone off to Canada to fight, and his mother and an older brother had kept the mill running. Thomas's daughter was also the daughter of the first Lucy Anne, whose father, Colonel Richard Hewitt, had been on the staff of General Hull at Detroit, and when, later, that general had been tried at court martial, he had been summoned as a witness. In those days there had been but one way to go east over the mountains, and that was on horseback; long before Colonel Richard Hewitt had reached Washington, the trial was over. He had come back to Ohio, left the army, and bought a farm. The sons and grandsons of these warriors of 1812 had fought in the Civil

War. All the young men of Margaret Baird's gener-
ation—she had had no brothers, but almost innu-
merable cousins—had been in the army. John Baird
himself had been with Grant at Vicksburg, had been
at Chickamauga and at Lookout Mountain, and had
marched through Georgia.

But the martial spirit of her ancestors was not
Lucy Anne's; she learned her history lessons duti-
fully but without enthusiasm. The wearisome reiter-
ation by her grandmother of these old stories, the
never-ending repetition of the names, Baird, Linley, Hewitt, had roused but little interest in them in
the child; it was all too long ago, and the battles had
been fought too far away. It was only when her
grandmother forgot that she was teaching history,
and touched upon something that had happened
there, in their own house, that Lucy Anne felt the
romance of the past. She was stirred to a delightful
quivering sense of strangeness, of the queerness of
time, when she could look about her and say
"Here—between these very walls. . . ." She had
been moved in that way by her grandmother's story
of her wedding. John Baird had come home from
the war on furlough, and they had been married in
the drawing room, the great front drawing room
that now had been given over for so long to darkness and dust. All the men at the wedding had been

army officers, and had worn full-dress uniform, including spurs, which had wrought havoc with carpets and draperies and hardwood floors. Grandmother's mother—the other Lucy Anne—had wept when the wedding was over—less because her only daughter had been married, and to a soldier who had almost at once to return to the field, than because her drawing room had been ruined. The other Lucy Anne had been a very beautiful, delicate-featured woman—there was a daguerreotype of her on the library mantel—the sort of woman who dies of a broken heart in poets' love songs—and there was something deliciously funny in the thought that she had been ordinary enough to care about carpets.

Lucy Anne's grandmother had been quick to feel the child's awakened interest. Nothing could have given her more pleasure. Battles were not really important to her either. Nothing was of importance except that Lucy Anne should be made to feel, unchangeably, that she belonged to her, to the Linleys, dead and gone, to the "Baird place." One afternoon when Lucy Anne asked her some eager question about her girlhood, she remembered that she had once kept a diary; she remembered a little leather-bound chest in the attic, a chest crisscrossed with strips of brass, studded with nails, that had not been opened since her husband's death. Her diary must be there, along with the one John had kept while he was at war, and the letters he had written her at that time, letters, too, from cousins and aunts, and those she had found in her mother's chest of drawers after her death, and had not liked to throw away.

She had this afternoon brought that chest down from the attic, along with the daguerreotypes of herself as a girl, of her lover and her cousins and her friends.

When Lucy Anne came in and squirmed into her seat at the library table, her grandmother handed her an American history, open at the pages that told of Lincoln's assassination.

"Before we begin, Lucy Anne," she said hurriedly, "I just happened to remember . . . in the old chest where I keep my diary that I wrote when I was a girl, and your grandfather's letters and his diary . . . I've got some copies of the papers that were printed the day after Lincoln was shot. Would you like to see them?"

"Grandmother—"

"If you would, say so, and I'll fetch them."

"I'd like to see the diary. The one that tells about when you were a girl."

"Very well. I'll get it—and the papers." She bustled out of the room, and bustled in again with the chest in her arms. Hilary had entered the room in her absence, and was lying on the couch. Her mother hesitated when she saw her, eyed her with disapprobation.

"We're having lessons. I wish you wouldn't interrupt."

"I shan't interrupt. May I not listen?"

Mrs. Baird set the chest down on the table.

"I suppose so. I brought some war-time newspapers down for Lucy Anne to look at."

"Oh, Gran!" Lucy Anne murmured reproachfully.

". . . And she thinks she wants to see my old diary. It's in here, too." Mrs. Baird unlocked the chest, threw back the lid, and removed the fragile, black-bordered newspapers. Beneath them were the two diaries. Her husband's she locked away in the table drawer: John's story of the war was not meant for babes. Her own she opened, with one hand, while she fumbled in her pocket for her spectacle case.

"Oh, dear, I've left my glasses somewhere. . . . Upstairs? In my room? Never mind—you can read it, Lucy Anne, out loud. I reckon it will be amusing to be reminded of those old days." She stole a glance at Hilary, and added politely, "unless it will disturb your mother."

47

"Not at all." Hilary's cool formality of tone matched her mother's, but she lifted one quizzical eyebrow. "I am sufficiently curious about old times, myself. If you are sure you don't mind Lucy Anne knowing how silly you probably were. Girls' diaries always do seem silly, fifty odd years after they were written."

"Of course I was silly. What girl seventeen—eighteen years old isn't? But it's too long ago for me to blush over it now. Go ahead, Lucy Anne."

Lucy Anne knelt in a chair by the table, and leaned over the little open notebook. Her grandmother's handwriting had changed but little since the entries had been made—had become only a trifle larger and more careless—and she had no difficulty in deciphering the minute and particular flourishes which filled the page before her. She began to read in the middle of the book:

"Sunday May 22nd, 1864

"Still quite warm. It did not rain for a wonder today, though we expected it to, as it was our Communion Day. There were quite a number out. How strange it seems with so many of our young gentlemen away. I do hope they will all live to get home again, if prayer will do any good for our armies they will certainly be protected, I know there

has many an earnest and heartfelt prayer been offered for them this day. Melissa came home with me to stay all night, what a beautiful bonnet she has, should love to have one like it. I wrote a letter to My Soldier."

Lucy Anne looked up at her grandmother through her lashes, a little abashed. Hilary, on the couch, was murmuring in her delight, "Oh, Mother, how perfect!"

"I told you it would be silly." Mrs. Baird was brisk, unsentimental. "Go on, Lucy Anne."

"But who was 'Melissa,' first?"

"Lissa Hewitt—Uncle Obadiah's and Aunt Margaret's oldest, and my best friend. Go on."

Lucy Anne complied.

"Monday May 23rd, 1864

"Very pleasant and warm till this afternoon when it blew up quite cool and we had quite a rain, but I had a chance to go fishing, so I went. Mary Jane, Nellie, Lizzie, Cousin Dave Thomas and myself, we went up to the Linley woods, had a very pleasant time till the rain came up, then we had to pile into the carriage, we had a gay time when we went to eat our supper, made the coffee, then all got into the carriage and ate our suppers and it rained

quite hard all the while. Nellie caught the only fish that was caught.''

> *''Tuesday May 24th, 1864*
>
> *''Rained again today but not quite so much, how nice it would be to have a few days without rain, but I suppose it is all for the best. Mother and I went over to Grandfather's this afternoon, had quite a pleasant visit. He does not look quite as bad as I expected, but he looks very bad. Saw Uncle John and Uncle Will. Aunt Rhoda is still staying to take care of Grandfather. I called this morning to see Lissa.''*

"Grandfather Richard Hewitt, the Colonel, that was, of course. He was eighty and over when he died in sixty-five. Just after I was married. Mother was the youngest of his family. . . . Go on."

> *''Friday May 27th, 1864*
>
> *''If it rained today I did not see it. It has been a very pleasant day. This afternoon I looked over some of My Soldier's old letters. Received the music I sent for, I believe it is quite a pretty piece if I could only play it. Nellie came up, she stayed to supper then she and Mother and myself went up in the graveyard. We came back, I went to the corner, then Mattie and Phoebe Wilson were there,*

Mattie came up with me, believe she knows some of the arrangements. *Lizzie and Frank called to see me."*

"Friday June 3rd, 1864

"*Splendid weather we are having—if the first three days rule the summer we must be going to have quite a pleasant one. This day has been a little long to me. This morning Mother and I went down to Aunt Rhoda's, had quite a pleasant visit, Lizzie is so funny. While we were away, Aunt Ella was here, I was real sorry it happened we were away. I would have loved to see her. Lizzie and I called at Cousin Priscilla's, Mother and Mary Jane followed us. Mattie was there. Lissa stopped at home for me then came down to Aunt Rhoda's. She came home with me for dinner, then she wanted me to go over to Auntie's with her to stay all night, but I feared I would not get home soon enough* tomorrow. *I bought me a veil, gave thirty-five cents for it, I think, it costs something to be a little fixed up. I believe Lissa and I could always get along together, she thought today had been very long too."*

"Saturday June 4th, 1864

"*A little cloudy at times, but a very fine day. The engine was out this afternoon. I saw the new one for the first time, how strange it seems to see so few men come with it. This evening saw J. for the first time in eighteen months, he is quite a* fine looking soldier—*was quite glad to see him—"*

"Oh, Mother! 'Quite glad,' forsooth!"

"I was glad—I remember that evening. We went to Mattie's and made taffy. Lissa was there, too, with her beau, and Lee and Nellie. Turn over to the next day, Lucy Anne."

"Sunday June 5th, 1864

"A very fine day, rather warm, but we cannot expect anything else this season, and it is getting pretty dry, too. Went to church with Lissa, we were both very sleepy. Saw Phoebe in her new bonnet, she looked very nice and sweet—"

"That was sarcasm, you see. Phoebe and I both wanted John Baird," his widow chuckled, "and consequently hated each other. Well—next?"

"We only had nine here for dinner besides our own family, Jennie, Kate and Rhoda, with Uncle Frank and Aunt Sarah, and Mary and Amanda with Uncle John and Aunt Ella. After dinner J. came stayed till about five or nearly, then called on Phoebe. This evening had to excuse myself from R. C. as I had another engagement for

the evening. I felt real sorry for him, but I could not help it, I was much better pleased with the one that was here, we had quite a confidential chat, *wonder what he thinks of me. He stayed till morning. He gave me another of his photos. I like it better than the last one."*

"Grandmother—that was here, *in this house?"* Lucy Anne lifted her elbows from the table, brushed her tumbled hair back from her face, and regarded her grandmother with her glowing black eyes.

"Of course, where else? It was my father's house."

"But where? The front drawing room?"

"More likely the front steps. Why?"

"I like to think about it—happening. And all these others—I know you were grown up when you wrote this—but did you know them when you were little?"

"Of course. They were all my cousins. Or most of them."

"And they all used to come here to play?"

"Of course."

"Oh, Grandmother! I wish I could get them all straight." Lucy Anne clasped her hands together prayerfully over the shabby old diary. "You know that Lancaster-and-York table in the history that shows what relation the kings were to each other? Couldn't you make a table like that of your cousins? Then when I read about them, I would know—"

Mrs. Baird cast an oblique triumphant glance aside at her daughter Hilary.

"If you are interested, I'd be glad to—only it must wait until tomorrow. There are pictures of most all of them in my basket of daguerreotypes, too. I'll get it out . . . but we must have our history lesson now. While I am getting supper you may go on reading the diary, if you like."

When Lucy Anne had gone to bed that night, her grandmother made the "table" of cousins; when, the next afternoon, the researches into the black chest were resumed, it was with the neat pages spread out before them on the library table, along with a selection from the daguerreotypes in the basket. The child was that day roused to more than passive curiosity, and herself dived into the chest and turned over the tied-up bundles of old papers. In a corner, she found half a dozen letters that had been thrown in loosely; she pulled them out.

They were written on a pale blue-gray paper, worn brown at the creases. They were not in envelopes, but folded together and sealed—the sealing wax still clung to the paper—and addressed on the blank side to "Mrs. Lucy Anne Linley." She opened one of them. It was signed "Catherine."

"Who was 'Catherine'? You didn't put her name in the table."

" 'Catherine'? Aunt Catherine Burns, I suppose. I forgot all about her. They all went out to Ioway when I was ten or eleven. She married that good-for-nothing Burns when she was very young, and they had forty-'leven children. I remember Mother's saying that finally Father forbade her to go to Aunt Catherine, or to have her here, because it always meant paying a lot of money to get them out of some scrape. But we always had one or more of the children here."

"Your mother must have been fond of her, though." Hilary, who was in the rocking chair by the window, dropped her sewing in her lap. "If her husband separated them, she probably cherished a grievance against him all her life. Or she wouldn't have saved the letters."

"She was fond of her. Catherine was her next older sister, and they had grown up together. . . . Read us one of the letters, Lucy Anne, and let's see what she said. . . . The writing is too spidery for me. . . . Look at the dates, and read the earliest one first."

55

Lucy Anne spread the letters out on the table and compared them.

"July the 3rd, 1852. July the 15th, 1852. The first day of September, 1852. September 25th, 1852."

"That was long before they went west, then. They lived somewhere in Union County, I think. Read the first one."

Lucy Anne read slowly, gravely, puzzling over the bad handwriting; and once she stopped to explain her hesitation: "She wasn't a very good speller."

"July the 3rd, 1852

"DEAR SISTER: This is a very bright day but I cannot enjoy myself. I am sick with grief and troubel in my old dayes. I have not eaten but one meal at the table since last Tuesday, and when I relate to you our misfortune, you will see that there is not any sorrow like my sorrow. Just think of the money we made when we sold that railroad right of way, and it is all gone and we are worse than nothing some two or three hundred dollars. The counstable was up on last Tuesday and he took everything but what the law allows us he stript the house of carpet and took the barrow and the spring wagon and left

56

us but one cow for this big family so you can juge how we fare we could not make enuf butter for us before and now we are out of butter more than half of the time they have taken our wheat in the field and our pigs in the pen and we have our flower to buy and our meat to buy and no money to buy with. Oh when I look at the naked floor O my heart melts and pours out like water to think that I worked day and night. Not a soul but me cut a rag and now I must do without a carpet. O I have cried till I cannot cry any more. My courage is fled and sumtimes I think I can't work any more, I once had the ambition of two women but it is all fled but you know I am compeld to work when I look at my little children that have to be reared up yet that would like to have everything like other girls and they must be debard on the account of a drunken father. If I could have kept half of that money from Jim and taken care of it we would have had plenty, and a home in the bargain even if it was only a bare farmhouse. But now I will give it up forever for we have got down under foot and we can never make a raise. I had twenty yards of carpet rolled up that never was cut out and they took that so you can know how I felt.

"I had to go to Brookville and warn all of the grogshop men not to let him have any more whisky and I learned that he treated fifteen in one place and how many more I can't tell so you can juge where the money goes. Me and the children can work and he will spend it and so we are destroyed from morning to evening. Sometimes I am most compeld to leave him then I think maybe he will do better but if he dont I will get the boyes to rent a farm and I will go with them but if he would quit drinking I would rather stay all together. All of the children are willing for to go with me and sum of the older ones have tried to persuade me to leave him but I know as soon as I leave him he is ruind for ever because I know that he thinks the world and all of his children and wife and as soon as they leave him he is undone for ever. So Dear Sister you see how I am hemd in on every side and I know not what to do. If I want to go to church I have to walk it is a mile and a half to Brookville the clostest place to go to church so you can juge I do not get there very often but the little ones go every Sabbath to Sabbath School and when they come home it makes three miles poor little tired roasted and hungry children. My little Mary Bell has been walking there once a week for her pianna lessons and every afternoon to do her practising her teacher let her use her pianna, but now no more lessons. It breaks her heart to give up her lessons. O just look how there is no calamity that a drunkard does not bring on a family he makes a slave of his wife of his children and of his beasts. You may think I am making a poor mouth so that Father will help me but no. I did ask him for a favor and he refused so I would starve before I would ask any more. Do not let him see this letter. O I do love my father and would like to see him every day if I could and all the rest of you. I feel now like I will never have the heart to come down. You must all come and see us tell Father to come up to see us. I have been very homesick and in the days of my affliction I remember all the pleasant things of the old times. Answer this letter Dear Sister. My love to you all.

"CATHERINE"

When she had finished reading the terrible letter, Lucy Anne looked from her mother to her grandmother and back again. Neither of them spoke. She took up the next one, dated July 15th.

"Dear Sister, as this is a pleasant evening I thought I could not spend any time more agreeable than to drop a few lines to you to tell you my joy and troubel. I am glad to say we are well I hope you are the same. I have been looking for you till my eyes have grown dim. I hope you have not forgot me tell Margaret I would like to see her. Dear Sister you have a home and you do not know how to simpathise with me we do not know where we will go to yet Jim talks some of going to Missura. Tell Brother Will that I would like to see him and the rest of them but you have all cast me to one side as an outcast and as such I feel. But a pleasing thought crost my breast. When we leave this unfriendly world we will part no more my tears will be dried up and I hope we will sing the song of Zion for ever.

"I was in hopes that I would get down to see all of you but at this time I do not expect to get down so this is How do you do and good by unless you come up.

"O sister, you know how I have worked hard for a home but my hope is blasted. It is no use to tell you what it is even if I could for you have heard. Jim thinks no one knows he drinks. Some dayes the teares are not dried out

of my eyes and midnight is a witness to my
teares. But so it is and I must make the best of
it. I hope it is for the best.

"CATHERINE

"O Lord may my companion leave off his eavil
habits so that we may live in peace together
with our children that we may meet on that
peaceful shore is my prayer."

Again Lucy Anne looked up. Her mother was
staring at her, her eyes softened, veiled.

"Oh, the poor woman!"

"She was a weak-minded, spineless creature,"
Mrs. Baird replied. "Why didn't she leave him? I
remember Father's asking that, when Mother
grieved for her. A woman of any character would
have."

"She tells you why she didn't. He would have
been 'undone,' and then they couldn't have 'met on
that peaceful shore' to 'sing the song of Zion for
ever.' I envy her her courage." Hilary paused for
a moment and faced her mother, who looked incredulous. "Yes—her courage—to face the consequences of her love and to—to 'bear it out even to
the edge of doom.' "

"Love!" Mrs. Baird's answer was an angry sniff. "Who could have loved a beast like Uncle Jim Burns?"

"She must have loved him—if she hadn't, she wouldn't have endured all that to save him from perdition. What a faith they had, those Victorian women!" Hilary's lips drooped sadly, a little scornfully.

"It seems to me I'd have stopped loving Jim Burns pretty quick."

"Mother, you never did know anything about love, really."

"Oh, I didn't! Didn't I put up with all John Baird's whimsies, and make him a good wife to the end of his days? Just because he was an ordinarily decent man, you think I didn't love him. Must one marry a scoundrel—?"

"On the whole"—the old sardonic gleam shone again in Hilary's eye—"on the whole, I think—yes. It is the only test."

"H'mph! Go on, Lucy Anne, let's have the rest of the letters."

"Oh, no, Lucy Anne. They are too terribly sad. Let the poor woman rest in peace."

"The next one is better." She had glanced at it while the others had been talking. "Her father bought her carpet back."

"The first day of September, 1852

"DEAR SISTER: I take the presant opportunity to inform you that we are all well but little Judy who has been quite sick since I came home. She is better now. I found them well and in good heart. Jim has done better since I came home and while I was gone Lydia said he did better. He has not been drunk as I know of since I came home but how long it will last I do not know. But we have got no place to go yet nor do I know of any place and I do not know what we will do if you hear of any farm to rent please let us know there are no farms around here for rent.

"I expect you miss me very much on the bread line do you not. Well I will tell you how you can get it back again just come up here and I will wait on you all with pleasure. We have four young turkeyes and I would as leaf you would help eat them up as anybody so Thomas come up.

"Lucy I have been wondering if you can tell me if any of the aunts or cousins would have Mary Bell come and stay for to help them and for company. Ask around and then write and let me know. It will be handy for school and she is willing to come down.

"When you get this letter write soon and tell me how you are getting along and when you got your quilt out and has Margaret started off to school? Judy has not forgot her if I say where is Margaret she will look all over to find her.

"I suppose you will enquire how I am satisfied since I came home well I can hardly tell you some dayes I am in pretty good heart and then some dayes are spent without hope. I am not quite so discouraged since my indulgent father has bought my carpet back again it cost twelve dollars thirty. You may know I take pleasure when I look and see my floor carpeted once more. I feel very grateful to my father for his kindness and also for your and Thomas's kindness. I can never pay you I am afraid but I send my regards to you all. Goodby for this time. Come up and see us. Bring Margaret with you so goodby once more.

"I remain your Sister with respect.

"Catherine Burns to Lucy Anne
and Thomas Linley."

"That must have been the winter that Mother had Mary Bell Burns come here. I can just barely remember it—it was my first year at school. She was going to be a music teacher, but she married instead and went to Missouri with her husband. . . . Are there any more letters?"

"One more. September twenty-fifth. It's a short one."

"DEAR SISTER, this pleasant morning finds me seated in my room in order to pen a few lines to let you know that we are all well and to answer your wellcome communication which should have been answered some time ago I expect you think I had forgotten you but I have been very busy making soap and I have many other excuses but let this suffice. Do not take an example of me when you receive this letter write as soon as you can for I am almost dead to hear from you and all the enquiring friends I do not expect that will be as many as none of you have been to see us this fall. I thought father would have been here before this but perhaps he thinks we have nothing to eat well sumtimes we have and sumtimes we have not but he should have the best we have. We had a good crop of buckwheat which comes very good. Our corn is about half bitten with the frost.

"I was very much gratified to hear from you and truly glad to hear that Mary Bell was satisfied. O Lucy and Thomas how good you are to my little girl she wrote me a letter about the pianna lessons and about your beautiful pianna inlaid with mother-of-pearl that you allow her to play on. I will direct my letter to her it will please her."

"There's a letter to Mary Bell on the other side of the paper, too."

"DEAR DAUGHTER, this pleasant Sabbath morning finds me seated in my room in order to pen you a few lines to let you know that we are all well at presant hoping these few lines may find you all enjoying the same blessing. I expect you think I have forgotten you but there is not a day passes but I think of you and I feel very much gratified to think that you have got such a good place I hope you will improve your time my little daughter you must treat your aunt as a mother be obedient to her help her along as much as you can for you know how kind her and your uncle was to us in a time of need.

"Your little schoolmates miss you very much they would like to hear from you. We can hardly wait till you answer this letter. You must write and tell us how your health is. My paper is full and so I will stop writing. I often think of you.

"Your affectionate mother

"CATHERINE BURNS"

"Was it on the *rosewood piano* that Mary Bell had lessons?" Lucy Anne was wide-eyed.

"Yes—it's the only piano we ever had. I had lessons on it, too, and hated them! I never could play, only just enough for the young men to sing to, when they came to call in the evenings."

"You told me not to touch it. I thought you were afraid it would be scratched."

"Scratched? No, it's you who would be scratched. . . . There, now," she added tartly, "let's say no more—"

Hilary laughed suddenly, a clear ringing astonished laugh. The other two stared at her.

"I never heard you come so near making an admission, Mother. . . . But your psychology is all wrong. Don't you remember how Miss Collins and you between you almost made me hate that piano? Just because you made me practice two hours every blessed sunshiny summer day?"

"But it wouldn't work that way in this case. I'm not so stupid. There's no use your trying to get around me."

"Mother, please, Mother," Lucy Anne interrupted their indirections. "Who was Miss Collins?"

"She was the village music teacher when I was your age—she lived in a little ramshackle frame house across the street from the court house. A desiccated little old maid. Does she still live there, Mother?"

"How should I know? I suppose so, and that she still gives lessons. She is the sort that doesn't die, but dries up and blows away at the age of ninety."

Lucy Anne, bent above the letters on the table before her, suddenly had a queer vision. Herself and a little old wrinkled yellow woman, talking on a street corner.

("Miss Collins, could you teach me to play the piano? My grandmother won't let me *touch* hers. I haven't any money for lessons, but when I am a musician I will pay you. Ask Mother, she will tell you that I am going to be a musician.")

Lucy Anne lifted her head, caught her mother's

eye. They stared at each other. Why had she heard herself say that, why had she known it, so positively? Her mother had never told her that some day she would surely be a musician. But her mother thought so. When, not how, mattered, then. She returned to another perusal of her great-great-aunt Catherine's sad letters.

Waking and sleeping that night, Lucy Anne's head was a whirl of dreams. There were children to play games with her: Lissa and Nelly and Mary Jane. The homely old-fashioned names made a music in her mind. Phoebe the enemy: Lucy Anne saw her a pretty child, blue-eyed and curly-haired. Old forgotten merriment and gaiety; there were echoes of it sounding, now that her ears were opened, from the walls about her. The echoes were tinged with sorrow, too, the pleasurable melancholy that only a child can fully enjoy: the melancholy of old unhappy far-off things. Catherine Burns, who would not leave her husband, and her hungry children. Through all the dreams there sounded, like the clear plangent note of a plucked harpstring the cry "and midnight is a witness to my tears."

3

AFTER BREAKFAST THE NEXT MORNING, WHEN HER MOTHER AND GRAND- MOTHER HAD SETTLED DOWN TO THE AC- complishment of the day's domestic duties, Lucy Anne crept away upstairs, opened the door to the Other Part of the house, and slipped through into the long corridor past the closed bedrooms. The Blue Room, the Green Room, the Guest Room, My-Father's-and-Mother's-Room (Thomas Linley's and his wife Lucy Anne's) and the Upstairs Sitting Room. She knew their names, because she had al- ways accompanied her grandmother in the spring-housecleaning progress through them. Now she opened no doors, but turned the corner of the hall and tiptoed slowly down the wide staircase. The dark rooms downstairs had lost most of their terror for her, because of the children who had played in them long ago. With the end of her pinafore she dusted off a corner of the lowest step and sat down against the newel post for the playing of her game.

It was easy now to people the dark with the friendly, laughing, graceful figures of little girls. Lissa and Nelly and Mary Jane. Even Phoebe. It lent zest to the game, this having a recognized enemy among them. And Phoebe looked *sweet* in her pale blue dress with the rows of ruffles on its full skirt, in her lace-trimmed pantalettes. (But she wasn't sweet, really. It was just her way.) The other little girls' full skirts and tight bodices were of printed calicoes, dun-colored, their pinafores black sateen, their shoes ridiculous tiny black slippers laced with ribbons across and around their ankles. Lucy Anne knew how they dressed because of her grandmother's daguerreotypes, and because of the pictures in *Little Women*.

The darkness in the hall was best for games of hiding. She and Lissa in the black corner under the staircase. Nelly in the cupboard at the end of the hall, whose door was so exactly like the panels on

either side of it. And Mary Jane (she was the bold-
est, the most daring of them all—she had bright
brown eyes and a tip-tilted freckled nose) Mary Jane
opened the lid of the long, black, carved chest
under the mirror—she crawled inside, and lowered
the lid on herself, all except for just a tiny crack.
Through the crack you could see a twinkling bright
eye.

("Oh, Mary Jane! Suppose the lid should come
tight shut, and you couldn't get out again!")

("Sh! Of course I can get out again. Don't tell
Phoebe!")

Phoebe darted around the hall searching for
them. She held her ruffled blue skirts up tight in her
arm to keep them out of the dust. She opened the
cupboard door, and Lucy Anne could see the pale
oval of Nelly's face in the obscure depths within.

("Nelly! You're caught! Come out here. Phew,
that's a dusty hole. I don't think much of your
housekeeping!")

("That's like you, Phoebe, to sneer. Never
mind—you don't know it now, but you're *not going
to get John Baird!*")

Phoebe could not find Mary Jane anywhere, and
finally gave up trying. With a sigh of weariness, she
spread the blue dress smooth beneath her and

slipped up on the top of the chest. The lid shut to with a snap.

("Oh, Phoebe! Mary Jane! She's inside!")

Lucy Anne started to her feet from her seat beside the newel post. Her heart thumped, she stared at the somber black chest, aghast. Suppose! Just suppose! She turned and raced up the front stairs, down the corridor, through the door that led into the back hall. Bright sunlight streamed through her bedroom door, and fell on the matting at her feet. She could hear the clatter of a dustpan somewhere downstairs, the swish of a broom, and she could breathe again. But what a game that had been!

After lunch, when she and her grandmother had endured with equal patience an hour's consideration of that most trying of subjects, arithmetic, they closed their books, returned to the diary and the daguerreotypes, and the stories of Margaret Baird's girlhood. Craftily, the child led her grandmother to talk of the games of the old days, and before she had done with her questions, she knew the rules and procedure of them all. "Ring-around-the-rosy," "blindman's buff," "drop-the-handkerchief."

On the next morning when her grandmother had gone outside to scold Aaron for something, Lucy Anne whisked through the dining room, across the back hall, through the door, and into the back drawing room. She was bolder today, and did not feel that she must creep down upon a possible danger slowly, step by step from above. Without hesitation, but on her tiptoes, she walked the length of the two rooms, under two chandeliers in their bags, past two yawning fireplaces, with the gold-framed mirrors above them—and then, not quite caring to look behind her, she reached out a trembling hand, unlatched the shutter and opened it. She turned and peered into the room.

The rosewood piano reflected the light from its gleaming dark surface, through all the dust motes that her passage through the room had set dancing, invisible until she had let the sunshine in. The rosewood piano. A sudden unaccountable pang shot through her. She caught her breath. Her mother, when she was a little girl, had learned to play it, and before that, her grandmother. When young gentlemen—young soldiers, of course—had come to spend the evening with grandmother, she had played songs for them to sing. Battle songs, perhaps. She had seen the names of such songs, somewhere. "John Brown's Body." "Tenting Tonight on the Old Camp Ground." "Just Before the Battle, Mother." . . . And still longer ago, when grandmother was still a baby, Mary Bell had had her lessons on that piano. Under its closed lid were the

mother-of-pearl flowers. Mary Bell had been a bashful, timid, frightened little girl, Lucy Anne thought,
because she knew that her father was a drunkard,
and at their house they hadn't always enough to eat,
but when she opened the piano lid, she forgot all
that. You would be sure to forget everything but
the music, if you could make music. Lucy Anne
knew that, because she had found that she could
forget everything, just listening. Listening to the
wind on a winter's night, listening to the birds at
sunrise on a summer morning, to the insects on a
hot August evening when she sat on the porch in the
dark, trying to distinguish them: the constant,
never-ending chirp-chirp-chirp of the crickets, that
made a background for the others: the locust's shrill
crescendo, the intermittent unmistakable call of the
katydid. Listening like that, you could let yourself
go, sinking down into space, until there was nothing
in the world but the sounds that reached your ears.

Lucy Anne stared at the piano, her fingers tight
in the palms of her hand, so that when she opened
them, little half circles were marked in the flesh.
What must it have felt like to be Mary Bell? Some
day she would play that she was—then she sighed
and relaxed—but not today. Today they were going
to play the games her grandmother had taught her
yesterday. "Drop-the-handkerchief." Lissa and

Mary Jane and Nelly and Phoebe were there with her—but five wasn't enough for "drop-the-hand-kerchief." Surely there were others who would come, if they only knew.

("Come with me, Lissa, let's look out the front door.")

Lucy Anne, in the hall, peered through the dusty side lights. Of course, there they were, coming up the driveway, swinging clasped hands between them, their muslin skirts blowing in the breeze. Mattie and Amanda, with Cousin Priscilla Hewitt, who was a little older than the rest, between them.

("How nice of you to come, just when we wanted you. You must all stay to dinner, it will only make seven extra besides the family. Just leave your hats there on the old chest. We are going to play 'drop-the-handkerchief.' ")

And then the front drawing room became a babel of laughter, a whirl of skirts. It was really quite enough to make you dizzy. You dropped your handkerchief behind Phoebe, out of politeness, though Lissa was your favorite, and after you had raced around the ring, you slipped into her place to catch your breath. Then Lissa had it, and you watched her, out of the corner of your eye, ready to pounce and swoop. When the lunch bell rang they were all breathless with laughing.

("Come on, all of you. Grandmother won't mind. There's always vittles enough for nine or ten extra.")

Lucy Anne untwisted her legs and climbed down from the shrouded dusty-smelling chair where she had been sitting, closed the shutters, and slipped back across the hall into the dining room.

After that, whenever the child saw her grandmother so busy that she knew she would not be missed, she slipped away into the drawing room, opened a shutter and curled up in one of the sheeted chairs to play her make-believe games. "Pussy-wants-a-corner." "Blindman's-buff." Then one morning she heard her grandmother call her. Hurriedly she closed the shutter and tiptoed through the creaking door into the back hall. Her grandmother was there, and in amazement confronted her.

"Whatever in the world?"

"I was just playing."

"But what can you play, in there in the dark?"

"I was just pretending. Pretending—" Lucy Anne stammered under the unimaginative eye of her grandmother. "Playing the games you told me about—with the little girls you told me about."

"Oh—but in there in the dark! It's all right, but

it seems to me a poor way to spend your time. You ought to be outdoors in the sunshine."

"It's easier in the dark. And that's where you used to play really. That made it easier, too. Don't you see?"

"In the drawing rooms? Indeed we weren't allowed to have our games in there. Those were always company rooms. We played outside on the terrace and under the trees."

Lucy Anne looked sadly crestfallen. It had all been wrong, then. The laughter and the voices— they were not really in the walls, after all.

"But never mind, now," her grandmother continued. "I called you because I thought you might like to go for a walk with Aaron."

"Oh, yes! I would." She had never been allowed to go anywhere with Aaron before, except just around the house.

"To the old church back yonder beyond the Old Farm. It's the church where your great-grandmother went when she was a little girl, and all her brothers and sisters."

"And didn't you?"

"No, because by the time I came along, the town had grown up from a crossroad settlement to be the county seat, and there was a bigger church there where we went. . . . Come along with me and get your sunbonnet. The sun is awfully hot this morning."

Lucy Anne followed her into the kitchen and accepted the sunbonnet from her hand.

"The old graveyard's there, too, but nobody's been buried there since they gave up the old church. Except Grandfather Richard Hewitt. His wife was buried there, in thirty-two, and he wanted to rest beside her. I've been thinking, lately, I ought to go over there and see what condition those graves are in. Just look, will you, while you're there, and see that the headstones are still standing? And if there are many weeds?"

She hurried out of the kitchen, Lucy Anne at her heels, and crossed the yard to the stable door, where Aaron was waiting.

"Just look over the fences, Aaron, around the church and the graveyard, and if there's any posts down or bars down, fix them up. I promised Mr. Brown when he rented the farm on that side that I'd be responsible for those fences, and if they're not kept up, the pigs will be in the graveyard."

4

L UCY ANNE WENT WITH AARON INTO A
WORLD SHE HAD NEVER SEEN BEFORE, EX-
CEPT FROM THE UPSTAIRS WINDOWS. FROM
behind the stable a rough wagon trail led across a
field, curved up and over a little round hill, and
dipped to cross a creek where three boards nailed
crosswise between two logs made the bridge. Beyond the creek the trail ended at a gate that opened
into a road, rutted, empty, white with dust.

Aaron unlocked the padlock on the gate, pulled
it open across a barrier of weeds, and, when they
had scraped through, sideways, he reached his arm

back, through the bars, hung the padlock on the chain again and snapped it shut.

"Aaron," Lucy Anne stamped her foot a little in the dust of the road. "Is this Baird land?"

"This here road? No, Miss. The road is public property. But on both sides, far as eye can reach, it all belongs to your grandma."

But high hedges and the roadside weeds shut off from Lucy Anne any view of the Baird land. She drew a long exultant breath, her senses alert to the new and different world into which she had stepped, side by side with Aaron. Not much of the world was visible. On either hand were the weeds, gray with dust, higher than her head. Bouncing Bet, Queen Anne's lace. Their leaves were curled under at the edges, brown and crackling with heat and drought. Behind the weeds were the taller hedges; they were gray, too, for there was no wind to stir the dust. But they were disturbed now and again; leaves were shaken, twigs thrust apart. Birds darted out, on hasty fluttering wing, bright-colored birds, but silent, except for gossipy startled chipperings.

Aaron pointed his crooked black forefinger at a cluster of wings in the dust ahead of them, active wings that belonged to plump, brightly speckled birds who were playing in the dust, bathing in it.

"Bobwhites," he explained. "Make mighty good eating, bobwhites, only it ain't lawful to shoot 'em."

The birds were awakened to their presence and scuttled away to the side of the road. From the depths of the hedge came the leisurely clear call: "Bob*white! Bobwhite!*"

"There now—just hear him calling. Reckon that's a bird you could whistle like, easy." Aaron pursed his lips and sent the answer back: "Bob*white!*" Then he turned to Lucy Anne.

"How come you ain't pestering me to sing for you no more?"

"Grandmother doesn't like singing. Not anybody's singing," she emphasized, embarrassed. "It isn't that she doesn't think your singing's good." Lucy Anne sighed. "She scolded me."

"Yes, ma'am? I tell you, honey, she sure got some quaint ideas, Miss Baird, yes ma'am." He nodded his head solemnly. "But she's treated this ol' nigger good, and he ain't going to annoy her none, no ma'am. So he ain't gonna sing where she's about, if she don't like it."

Silently, after that, they walked down the road. The dust rose about them, and slowly, stirred by some faint current of air, drifted over the fields and hung there, or settled on the weeds and the hedges. The road twisted uphill; ahead of them there was nothing to be seen but blue sky, pale in the intensity of light. Everything was pale, Lucy Anne thought, veiled in heat and light and dust, except for the birds. She listened for them in the hedges.

"Now—just over the hill, and we're there." Aaron urged her on. The tops of trees, dim-colored like everything else, had become visible over the hill. A little further along and they could see the squat little steeple among the branches.

The church and the graveyard were set back from the road for several yards. The road branched. The branch that led to the church was washed into deep cracks, dry and hard; weeds grew through all its length. Walking on it was almost like walking on a plowed field.

"You just play 'round to suit yourself, now, while I look after the fences. But don't go over into the fields, because they're full of pigs, and maybe cows."

Lucy Anne had no desire to wander in the fields. She walked up close to the church and stared at it. It was like a square whitewashed brick box, not nearly so large as their empty stable. The whitewash had peeled off in spots; the windows were boarded over. Holes in the roof showed where shingles had blown off, and the unpainted wooden steeple was a weathered gray.

Here had Linleys and Hewitts and Bairds gone to church, once upon a time. (Lucy Anne had read about "going to church" in her grandmother's diary.) But somehow she could not make it seem real. It was all too long ago. Except for Colonel Richard Hewitt, she did not even know the first names of any who had lived so long ago. They were not important, anymore. It was terribly sad, to have lived so long ago as that. So that not even your name mattered anymore, and the places where you had been were allowed to fall to pieces, because no one cared that they had once been your places. But her great-great-grandfather Colonel Richard Hewitt had cared, until he had died. It had been important to him to be here, because his wife had been here—was here, in the graveyard.

She turned away from the church, and found the gate into the graveyard; she could not open it, it was too fast-set in earth and grass and weeds, but she could pull it away from the post at the top until there was room for her to squeeze through.

The graveyard was an uncomfortable place for walking. There were burrs and beggar's lice, and blackberry vines sprawled everywhere to trip you up and scratch your legs and hands, and the ground was treacherously soft, and gave beneath your feet. Lucy Anne shivered and stood still for a minute; she

felt a horror of the soft earth, letting her down. . . .
From the farthest corner of the little square of
ground, yucca had spread and overgrown half the
graves. Yellow, lichened, crumbling headstones
leaned on the gray-green leaves. Lucy Aaron knew
the plant—Spanish bayonet, Aaron called it—there
was a clump of it on each side of the terrace steps—
but she had never seen a place where it had taken
possession as it had here. It was more like swords
than bayonets, though. Like swords thrust forth by
an unfriendly earth. Lucy Anne stared about her,
transfixed by the macabre idea. Swords thrust forth
through bodies that the worms were eating. The
earth did not want corruption buried beneath its
grasses. Its friendly green comfortable grasses. It
was almost like a song, she thought, a terrible song,
singing itself in her mind. She remembered a verse
in the Book of Job that she had read not long ago
to her grandmother. "I said to corruption, thou art
my father, to the worm, thou art my mother and my
sister." The sunlight seemed to grow paler, more
intense, until the whole world quivered in a haze.
There was something blasting and deadly in the
heat. Lucy Anne turned away from the yucca and
ran tripping through the blackberry vines, until she
found herself leaning on a tilted white slab of marble. She drew her hand away from the hot head-

stone as if it had really burned her, but she stooped to read the still clearly incised letters that were on it. It was the only white stone in the graveyard, and looked the least aged. And it was her great-great-grandfather's. Richard Hewitt, born 1780, died 1865. Beside it there was another like it, but older. The letters had been almost obliterated by moss and lichen, but she could read them: Elizabeth Lane Hewitt, wife of Richard Hewitt. Born 1785, died 1832.

How long ago! Oh, how terribly long ago! And now the yucca, like swords in the earth, sending its roots where hands had been folded to rest forever!

Lucy Anne felt suddenly out of herself—not herself—but old—old—old as Elizabeth Hewitt, who had been here so long; she felt herself singing—singing for all the world to hear about the yucca swords in the old graveyard. But she did not sing. With a white face she struggled through the burrs and the blackberry vines, back through the gate that was loose on its hinges but fast-held by weeds and earth.

Aaron was at work near by, nailing up a bar of the fence with the hammer he had carried with him. He looked up and called to her.

"Rest yourself somewheres out of the sun. I'm almost ready to start back."

She sat down to wait on the worn stone doorstep of the church. Now that Aaron's voice had sent her gruesome thoughts flying, she was sorry that she had not waited longer in the graveyard. The little yellow, crooked stones beside the two marble ones—whose graves had they marked?

And where were the Linleys? Were they buried somewhere here, Thomas Linley's father, who had built the mill in the wilderness, and his wife, who had kept the mill grinding corn while he was fighting, away in the north somewhere? They should be here, because all the land around and about, that belonged to her grandmother now, had come to her from the Linleys, and not from Colonel Richard Hewitt. And what of John Baird's two grandmothers and grandfathers? Where were they? She began to feel confused at the thought of all the great-great-grandfathers and mothers that were behind you. Eight. No, not eight—sixteen. She sprang to her feet in the excitement of the thought. These were only her mother's people, here. And her father's? Her heart beat tumultuously, her thoughts leaped ahead of her, piled up, tumbled away—she could not sort them out. Her father's father's fathers. Who were they? She did not even know that. And she dared not ask; she was never to mention her father again. Perhaps they had all been—vagabonds. And perhaps it was better not to know. She trembled at the thought of a past so dark, so haunted, that it was better curtained.

Once again she sat down on the doorstep, her arms clasped about her knees. It was better, after all, to think of Colonel Richard Hewitt and his wife Elizabeth. A brave soldier against Indians and the British redcoats. He had ridden east to Washington on horseback. He had had many children and many grandchildren and some great-grandchildren before he died. A kind old man, and good to them all. Why, of course, Lucy Anne thought, and opened her black eyes wide as she stared across the fence at the blackberry-covered grave: Colonel Richard Hewitt was "my indulgent father" who had brought back Catherine Burns's carpet for her, for twelve dollars and thirty cents. Where were all the Burnses now, she wondered. Catherine and her husband buried somewhere in Iowa. Mary Bell and her husband buried somewhere in Missouri. But perhaps not. Mary Bell had not been so very much older than Grandmother. Perhaps she wasn't dead, but living with her grandchildren somewhere.

It was to a little country church just like this one, but in Union county, that Mary Bell and her brothers and sisters had walked for Sabbath School. A mile and a half there, and a mile and a half back.

Aaron came around the corner of the church, swinging his hammer in his hand.

"I'm through. Come along now. You'll have to step right smart or you'll be late for your dinner."

(Poor tired children, Lucy Anne was thinking. A mile and a half, now, home to dinner. Would there be any dinner today? Maybe not. Or perhaps there was enough of the buckwheat flour left. Surely mother would find something for her poor roasted hungry children.)

Lucy Anne ached for Catherine Burns, who had had so many children, and had loved them so well. Perhaps you wouldn't mind going without your dinner once in a while, if you were Catherine Burns's little girl. She would try playing at being Mary Bell Burns for the mile and a half of blazing hot road that lay ahead of them.

("Come on, little Judy, take my hand, and don't whimper. We'll soon be home now, Richard—" Surely one of them would have been named for his grandfather. "Richard, please be nice, and take her other hand. She's so little. It's wicked to chase the birds, anyway.

("Now, Judy, keep your sunbonnet on, or you'll be sunstruck. And you mustn't try to hurry—we'll be there soon enough. See—we're at the top of the hill already. Look back, and you'll see how far away the church looks, now. Oh—*look* out! Help her, Richard. There's a carriage coming!")

Because of course almost everyone who went to the little church must have had carriages. She could hear one passing, as she trudged along beside Aaron, her eyes on the dust-filled ruts ahead of her. The horse's feet went clop-clop-clop. The wheels squeaked a little on the hubs. There were voices of men, and ladies laughing. The dust came up in choking clouds behind them.

("Don't cry, Judy. They weren't laughing at us. I'm sure they weren't. And they would have taken us in with them to ride part of the way home, if our feet hadn't been so dusty. Don't you see they couldn't? We'd have spoiled their silk-Sunday dresses. Richard, can't you carry Judy piggyback for a little way? She's so *tired!*")

They came, Lucy Anne and Aaron, to the gate in the hedge that would lead them back across the fallow land where the asters and the black-eyed Susans were in flower, and over the narrow bridge across the creek, and through the sweet-corn patch and the vegetable garden.

("Put her down now, Richard. She can walk the rest of the way. It isn't so dusty. And I tell you—let's take Mother some of the asters and black-eyed Susans to put on the table.")

Lucy Anne darted away from Aaron and gathered handfuls of the bright prickly-stemmed flowers. He remonstrated with her.

"What you-all want with them old weeds? Plenty of 'sturtiums and marigolds right outside your window."

("That's enough, Judy. Poor Mother didn't have time to plant any flowers this summer, with the constable in the house, and all. Now, we've only to go over the creek and past the cornfield and the vegetable garden and we'll be there. Mother will be waiting in the door.")

The stable door, because probably the uncarpeted house the Burnses had lived in wouldn't have been any larger than the Baird stable. But while she cheered Judy on, she knew that in a minute she would have to be Lucy Anne again, and that her mother would not be waiting in any door.

But her grandmother was—in the kitchen door. Lucy Anne gave her the flaming, acrid-scented flowers, and wiped the prickliness out of her hand on her sock.

"Thank you, honey. Did you have a nice walk?"

"Yes, Gran. But it was dusty."

"Take this rag and dust your feet off before you come in."

Lucy Anne pushed her sunbonnet back on to her

shoulders and wiped off her streaming face, then she flicked at her shoes with the rag.

"Poor lamb! Your face is scarlet. Was it as hot as all that? Are you tired?"

"Tired and roasted and *hungry*. Are there buckwheat cakes for dinner?"

"Buckwheat cakes! In this kind of weather!"

Lucy Anne laughed. "I've been thinking of buckwheat cakes all the way home."

5

IN THE MORNING, SHE WOULD BE MARY BELL BURNS AGAIN; SHE WANTED TO KNOW WHAT IT FELT LIKE, LEAVING YOUR MOTHER, CATHerine Burns, and your little sister Judy and all your other brothers and sisters, to come here to be with your Aunt Lucy Anne Linley.

And so, on the next day, she stole away again from her grandmother and opened the door into the drawing room. Perhaps children did not play games in here, but Mary Bell must have come in to help her aunt with the dusting.

Lucy Anne moved disconsolately from one massive sheeted piece of furniture to another. There was a tremendous lot of dusting to be done: sofas and chairs and what-nots. It was easier at home, where there weren't even any carpets, and where there were lots of sisters to help. You were never alone at home, and here there was only Aunt Lucy Anne's little girl Margaret to play with.

Then in her progress through the rooms, Lucy Anne came to the rosewood piano.

(Oh, the piano! She remembered: that is why Mary Bell is here. At home there isn't any piano, and no money to pay for lessons. But here—)

(Inside the lid, the piano is inlaid with mother-of-pearl. And of course it must be dusted.)

Lucy Anne stepped close to it, ran her finger over the narrow band of carving around its base, then braced herself and cautiously raised the lid, folded its leaves together, and laid it back. Behind the keys curled a vine of roses inlaid into the wood, with mother-of-pearl petals and mother-of-pearl leaves. The keys were half of them black as ebony, half of them a warm yellow-white, almost the color of her fingers. She spread her hands on the keys to compare them. Quite accidentally, the little finger of her right hand came down too hard and depressed the last yellow key. The piano gave forth a high, soft, blurred note. A pale note, a little veil of sound, ghostly and haunting.

The startled child thrust her hands behind her and stared at the drawing-room door. But nothing happened. Her grandmother couldn't have heard that little soft echo of a sound. Again, with her little finger, she touched the key. The note was what the sun had been, for a moment, yesterday, in the graveyard, when she had stood staring at the yucca: pale and blurred, a veil through which the world moved tremulous and dizzy. Perhaps she could find a note that would be sharp and swift and keen, like the leaves of the Spanish bayonet. Cautiously, gently, she pressed the keys in succession, until she found the one she wanted. Twice she played it. It should have been clear and sweet and piercing, but it jangled a little, set her teeth on edge. However, hadn't the leaves like sword blades done just that? She played the two keys together: the sun and the yucca; the yucca whose roots were thrust between bare rib-bones, because the earth did not want them there. She must find a note for the roots of the yucca, deep in the earth. On down the piano she moved. The notes became less ghostly, less blurred. She found one that rang hollow, a profound disquieting tone. It would do. By stretching, she could play the first two keys with one hand, the third with the other, and when she played them all together, she would have a little song about the graveyard.

The music they made, the three keys together, was strange and eerie. It made her shiver, just as the graveyard had done. At the sound of a door squeaking on its hinges, she cried out, and looked over her shoulder apprehensively.

Her vague fears gave way to a definite one. Her grandmother was standing in the drawing-room door. Lucy Anne tried hurriedly to close the piano lid, but her fingers trembled, and the lid came down with a bang. She hardly dared to look up. When she did, she saw her grandmother pale and startled in the dusky room. For a moment there was silence.

Then "What were you doing?" her grandmother asked. She must have known, of course. It was as if that were the only thing that could be said at first, as if all the other things had to wait until she was less startled, and could be said calmly. Perhaps her grandmother hoped they wouldn't have to be said.

Lucy Anne, strangely, wanted to reassure her, to comfort her.

"It wasn't me, Gran. It was Mary Bell Burns."

"What? What do you mean?"

"I mean, I was pretending to be Mary Bell Burns, having her music lesson." It wasn't fibbing exactly.

She had been pretending, until she had played the first note, and had forgotten.

"I see. And while you were pretending, did you forget that I had forbidden you to touch the piano?"

Lucy Anne could not honestly say that for a moment she had forgotten such an important thing as that.

"No. Gran. I didn't forget."

"Then you deliberately disobeyed me?"

"It wasn't me, I tell you. It was Mary Bell Burns."

"I have never known you to be disobedient before." Her grandmother lifted her hand from the doorknob and began to smooth down with her palm the neat crisp waves of her white hair. "I think I had better lock this door. Then you won't come in here."

"Oh, Gran!" Lucy Anne would have begun to whimper, had not her mother just then appeared, outside the door, behind her grandmother. The child stiffened, clasped her hands hard behind her back. She could not have whimpered in the presence of her mother. She stood silent, waiting, beside the piano.

Hilary looked into the room, and laughed, suddenly, briefly.

"So," she said, "the tiger has tasted blood?"

"Hilary," her mother turned, "will you please go back and leave me to handle this?"

"Certainly. It is your affair—yours and Lucy Anne's." With a strange smile, she shrugged her shoulders, turned and disappeared. The child sighed, and relaxed. Her mother knew everything: what she had felt and why, but she would not help her. She was left with only her own perhaps impotent weapons against her grandmother. She prepared for tears. But her grandmother saw the rising storm, and fortified herself.

"Lucy Anne, disobedience is a serious thing to me, no matter in what way you disobey." (There was a weakness in that statement, because, somehow, Lucy Anne knew that other disobediences would have seemed trifling, compared to this.) "Only headstrong little children disobey deliberately and intentionally, and if you are going to behave like a little child, you must be treated like one. I want you to go upstairs, undress and go to bed. And no tears. The more childishly you behave, the longer you will stay there. If you go quietly, you may get up tomorrow morning, just as usual, and go on as if this hadn't happened. But you will find this door locked."

Lucy Anne was stunned into a silent acquiescence. She had never been sent to bed in her life before. Without a word, she passed through the door under her grandmother's arm, marched steadily through the house to the back stairs, plodded up the stairs and into her bedroom. Her grandmother followed, and grimly, without a word, turned back the bedcovers, drew her nightgown from under the pillow, shook it out, and laid it over the back of a chair.

"Now let me see you get into that quickly."

With numb fingers, Lucy Anne struggled with her buttons. Her grandmother stood over her, waiting, but did not offer to help. She slipped her clothes off, dived into the nightgown, and then sat down on the edge of the bed to unbutton her slippers. Tears were streaming down her cheeks. She wiped them off hurriedly on the bosom of her nightgown.

"Oh, Grandmother! Must I stay here all day? Can't I even have anything to read?"

"No. I want you to lie here and think over the consequences of disobedience."

"Can't I even have anything to eat?"

"Of course," her grandmother snapped. "You won't be starved, whatever you do."

Lucy Anne rolled over into the bed, buried her face in the pillow, drew the sheet over her ears. Her grandmother left the room. When the door had closed, she turned over, wiped the last of her tears on the ruffles of the pillow slip, and folded the edge of the sheet neatly back beneath her chin.

Inside the house, all was silence. Through the open windows she could hear the lawn mower on the terrace. That would be Aaron. If she let herself go, so that her mind had nothing to do but listen to the sounds that reached her ears, she could hear . . . she could hear, away way off somewhere, the voices of children and a dog barking. A horse's hoofs on the distant street. The thin insistent cry: "Swe-et corn to-*day*. . . ." It was queer how, the more you let go, the more sounds you could absorb, from farther and farther away. But it wouldn't do to let yourself go too far. She roused herself, abruptly. She did not like her strange feeling that all the world had changed, suddenly. But perhaps it was only because she had never been in bed in the day-time before.

Disobedience. That was what she was in bed for. She might as well really disobey, then. She began to sing softly, "Go down, Moses." But after all, she had promised her grandmother that if she found herself singing, she would stop. She tried to make herself forget that she was now singing "Go down, Moses," but she could not quite manage it. And breaking a promise was worse than doing something you had never said you would not do, even if it had been forbidden you. The song died on her lips.

If only her grandmother had not come into the drawing room just when she did. In a little while she would have had a song all her own. She remembered the three notes: she spread her hands out on the sheet as on the piano keys.

Why had her mother said "The tiger has tasted blood"? Lucy Anne knew quite well what her mother meant. You often did know what she meant even when she had said nothing at all. That other afternoon, for instance, when she had known that her mother knew that she was going to be a musician, when neither of them had said a word—had only looked at each other. But "the tiger has tasted blood"—that was queer, because she wasn't a tiger, and how, if her mother knew what went on inside of her head, could she think that she was? Who could expect a tiger to be obedient? A tiger would get what it wanted.

She remembered Miss Collins, suddenly. That was what she wanted. She would meet her on a street corner, and she would know her because she was little and yellow and dried up, and looked as if the wind might blow her away. And she would say: "Miss Collins—"

Her fantasy was interrupted by her grandmother's entrance with a loaded tray. Lucy Anne sat up in bed and ate a hearty meal, while her grandmother, in the rocking chair beside her, waited for the tray. There was no conversation. That, of course, as Lucy Anne understood, was part of the punishment.

After she had finished, and her grandmother had taken the empty dishes, and had closed the door behind her, she lay back on her pillows and prepared to resume her conversation with Miss Collins. But she found herself out of patience with purely imaginary activity. Perhaps the solid reality of the hot dinner she had eaten had changed her outlook. She felt more tigerish. What if she were *really* to go, now and at once—?

Suppose she dressed and slipped out of the house, over the fence and away. Disobedience, again. If she were caught, she would have to go back to bed. But she should be able to find Miss Collins and get back before her grandmother came up with her supper tray. And she would not try to find her on a street corner; she would ask someone to point out her house, and she would go and knock on the door.

"I am Hilary Baird's little girl, Lucy Anne. You remember that you gave her music lessons once?

And my father was a musician, too. Could you give me lessons? I haven't any money, and neither has mother, and grandmother won't pay you because she doesn't want me to be a musician. But when I am one, then I will pay you."

Suppose Miss Collins refused? She might not like a little girl—a tiger—who disobeyed her grandmother. It seemed likely, but unless she asked her, she would never know.

Grandmother and Mother would be in the kitchen now, washing the dinner dishes. And from the kitchen windows you could not see the back hall door.

Lucy Anne slipped out of bed and into her clothes; the buttons went into the buttonholes with magic ease. She dared not take the time to unbraid her long plaits and brush and braid them up again; she took the brush and smoothed her hair down over her ears. Then, with thumping heart she opened the door and listened. She could hear the dishes rattle in the kitchen. She crept down the stairs, along the hall, and opened the outside door. Nothing happened. On the doorstep she closed it behind her, releasing the knob slowly so that it would make no noise. On hands and knees she crept around the house, through the sweet-smelling grass blades that Aaron had cut that morning, to the *porte-cochère*.

On the driveway, she began to run. They could not see her now. It was a long way to the gate, and she reached it gasping and out of breath, but she did not pause nor hesitate. She flung herself at it, seized hold of the bars, and began to climb. At the top there were spikes, tipped like arrows, but she could get over.

Stooping precariously on the next-highest bar of the gate, she paused to glance at the outside world. Except for the continuous and therefore unnoticeable chirping of the crickets it lay silent under the heat of the midday sun. She had heard nothing to startle her, and at first saw nothing but the shimmering heat waves that hung over the cement sidewalk. But when she turned her head to look down the street, there was the figure of a man—a man not merely passing by, but waiting, and watching her, smiling. Not since she could remember had she spoken to any man, save Aaron. She forgot the cool audacity of the plans she had made. After a second's pause, she caught her breath with a frightened little exclamation, let go the spiked top of the fence, and leaped backward into the safety of the tall grass behind her. But the hem of her dress caught on one of the spikes; she was thrown with an awkward jerk

into a tumbled heap on the ground. With an ago-
nized cry she attempted to rise, then dropped back
again, dizzy and breathless with pain, a crumpled
knot of gingham dress, out-thrown arms and long
black braids of hair.

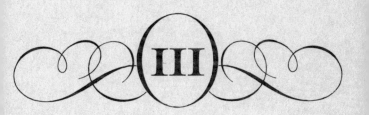

1

O N THAT SAME SUNNY NOON, DR. MAR-
TIN CHILD HAD RISEN FROM HIS SOLI-
TARY LUNCH AND HAD STROLLED OUT
into the heat of the day. He had felt it impossible
to shut himself in his office for the afternoon, with
a succession of querulous patients, until he had been
washed clean in the furious heat of the sun. He
found himself alone on the streets. He turned away
from the center of town and into the North Road;
he walked slowly past the Baird place, his hat pulled
over his eyes, watching the grasshoppers at his feet
as they became aware of his approach. The shrilling,

jubilant voice of each in its turn ceased; a little wave of silence preceded him. One after another drew up its legs, poised, and hopped into safety in the weeds. He avoided treading on the few who leaped lucklessly in the wrong direction.

With his mind on the small things of the summer world, like grasshoppers, he only absent-mindedly paused at the driveway gate, and looked up. Between the bars he saw Lucy Anne as she came running. Like one in a forest, fearful of startling a wild creature—a fawn, bounding through the underbrush—he stopped in his tracks. While he watched, she hurled herself on the bars of the gate, and began to climb. Then when she looked up and saw him, and her face paled with fright, he felt suddenly compassionate—eager to explain his good intentions, but helpless—again as one feels towards a startled fawn. But when he saw the leap backwards, and the twisted fall, he smiled. "Poor little grasshopper!" And still he waited. Her cry drew him to the gate, and he peered in.

"God bless my soul!" he thought. "The helpless babe—she has actually hurt herself." She lay without stirring where she had fallen, her face buried in the grass, her arms above her head.

He swung himself over the gate, dropped at her side, touched her on the shoulder. Still she did not move. He put his hands under her and turned her over, and her head fell back limp against his arm. He saw the twisted foot, doubled beneath her. A broken ankle. He pulled her sock down and moved the foot gently, to make sure, while she was still only half conscious. . . . He must carry the child to the house.

When he had risen with her in his arms, and started off on the dim green-shadowed way that curved between the maple trees, he looked again at the face that lay in the crook of his arm, and suffered a swift revulsion of feeling. This dark, elusive, timid creature—she could have nothing in her of Hilary Baird. He had dreamed that through the child he might some day reach her—but he had forgotten the child's Latin father. The thought repelled him. The two thick braids of black hair that hung swinging over his arm repelled him—the black hair that unplaited, must have been like a lustrous cloak about her shoulders. Hilary's hair was black, too, but soft, not weighted with Latinity, like this. He saw the full pure oval of the child's face, the bow of her mouth that rose to meet the short upper lip, the dusky pallor of her face, like a magnolia flower that has been under the rain (a translucent pallor, drained of color). The blue veins, minute but clear, were distinct on her temple, the eyebrows were perfectly arched, the lashes long and curled and black. She was a beautiful child, this daughter of Hilary Baird, but through her you could feel your way back, not to Hilary but to far places and other people—to olive-clad hills, to narrow clamorous streets and bridges over the Arno. Here she was alien—alien and strange.

Then Lucy Anne opened her eyes and looked up at him. Her eyes were midnight black, unfathomable under the mist of tears that lay on them and on her lashes. There was pain in them, and terror. He saw the moving heartbeats at her throat, but she did not shrink from him, nor twist in his arms. She dropped her lids again and lay passive.

They were still beneath the low green branches of the maple trees, in an unreality of shadows and cool unstirring air. It was that, perhaps, that made him think as he did: "Not his, after all. His no more than Hilary's, but a changeling, of some dim twilight faerie world." Then he laughed at himself for a fanciful fool, and spoke to her gently, as physicians speak.

"You are not afraid of me now, are you? You hurt yourself when you jumped, you know, and I am a doctor and will make it well."

She opened her eyes again, searched his face, and smiled a little, through her tears.

"Must you?"

"*Must* I?" he repeated, surprised.

"Couldn't you put me down and let me go back and not tell anyone?" An embarrassed flush crept into her cheeks, warmed her pallor.

"I'm afraid I couldn't. So you were running away, were you, and don't want anyone to know? But you hurt your ankle, don't you remember, and couldn't stand. Doesn't it hurt now?"

"Some. But it's mostly numb, like being asleep. If I could stand, I'd rather it would hurt than tell Grandmother. She will put me back to bed."

"So that's it." He laughed. Faerie changelings, he believed, were always mischievous and unmanageable. "But I am afraid you will have to go back to bed anyway, my dear child. You've broken the bone, and it will take a long time to heal."

She began to cry then, in earnest. She gave up the idea of fighting the pain, concealing it.

"Is it worse? Why do you cry now, when you didn't before?"

Then Dr. Martin looked up and saw Aaron in the path before them.

"Whut you doin' with huh, suh? Don' yuh know Miz Bai'd don' 'low no strangehs—"

"Hush, man! She's had an accident. You go ahead of us and tell your mistress the little girl has broken her ankle, and ask them to get ready for her."

The dismayed Aaron touched his hat. "Yas, suh, yas, suh. Ah'll do so." He turned and shambled off. "Jes' follow me, suh."

Dr. Martin followed him, around the side of the house. He was roused to pardonable curiosity, and rejoiced that he had been outside the gate when she fell. But he corrected himself sternly: if he had not been there it would not have happened. He wondered where the child had been running.

Both Hilary and her mother had come to the door at Aaron's summons. Mrs. Baird cried out in dismay.

"But Lucy Anne! What were you doing out of bed?"

Hilary was quicker than her mother. She opened the screen door and motioned the doctor inside.

"I am Dr. Martin Child. You see, I saw her fall—"

"Her ankle, Aaron said? Can you carry her upstairs?"

"Oh, put her in my room, Hilary."

"It isn't necessary. You'd be upset if you were turned out, and had to sleep in a strange bed, and where she's put, she will have to stay!"

"But if you have a couch downstairs," the doctor

interrupted, "I can set her ankle before I carry her up."

Hilary led the way through the hall, and showed him the couch in the library, and he laid Lucy Anne on the cushions as gently as possible.

"May I send the colored man to Dr. Mason's hospital for splints and bandages? He should be able to get there and back in fifteen minutes."

"Certainly."

"Then watch her, will you, to see that she doesn't move, while I write a note?"

"There are pens and paper on the table there." Hilary moved over to the couch, and Mrs. Baird went outside to call Aaron.

When he had gone, Dr. Martin took Hilary's place at the foot of the couch. He took off her slipper and, with the scissors he had found in Hilary's open work basket, he cut the sock into shreds. Then holding her leg firmly in one hand, with the other he moved her foot again, slowly and tenderly. Lucy Anne screamed.

"There's no doubt about it. A fractured fibula. You can feel the ends of the bone grate on each other," he explained. He looked up at Mrs. Baird, beside him. There was a white line around her lips.

"Go outside, Mother, and wait. This will hurt you more than it will Lucy Anne, if you stay to watch, and there is nothing you can do. . . . Or, better still, go up and make her bed." Hilary laughed as she turned back to the doctor. "You see, she was supposed to be in that bed."

Mrs. Baird hurried out of the room, her hands twisted together under her apron. Dr. Martin told Hilary how he had watched Lucy Anne climb the gate, and how he had seen her fall. The child lay silent, breathing heavily through the long minutes that passed so slowly, until Aaron came in again, with splints and bandages. Then Hilary rose and stood close to her.

"This is going to hurt, Lucy Anne, but I will stand here beside you, and if you will try not to cry, I will hold your hand."

Lucy Anne opened her eyes in amazement and smiled at her mother. Dr. Martin noted her expression, as he bent above the ankle, but he could not give room in his mind now to consideration of that strange glance between the two. He pulled the bone into place and held it. There was only one low anguished exclamation from the child. He guessed that she was twisting her mother's hand in hers, but she shed no tears. Hilary smiled at her, touched the black hair gently with her other hand, and released her fingers from Lucy Anne's grip that she might help the doctor with the bandages. As she held them in place, he was startled when he felt for an instant the heat in her fingertips, but he could not consider that now, either.

When, finally, he had done, and Lucy Anne lay white and limp on the couch, her leg in its framework, he straightened and turned to Hilary.

"Now, I'll carry her upstairs, if you will show me the way."

"Certainly. But I think she had better go in my room, after all. She'll have to be there so long—and there's a porch outside, with a door. It's airier, in this hot weather."

He stooped again over Lucy Anne; she put her arms around his neck, and he picked her up and followed Hilary across the hall, and up the stairs into her bedroom.

Mrs. Baird came from Lucy Anne's door where she had been waiting, and followed them. He put the child down on the edge of the wide four-poster bed.

"I'll leave her to you to undress—"

"How long"—Lucy Anne spoke for the first time since he had brought her in—"how long must I stay here?"

"In bed? Only a few days, I hope. But it will be a long while before you are climbing fences again, young woman."

"You see, now," Mrs. Baird cleared her throat hoarsely, "you see what happens to little girls who disobey."

"I hadn't promised."

"Promised?"

"Don't scold, Mother. She forgot that I had promised, for her."

Mrs. Baird said "H'mph," and bustled angrily out of the room. The doctor looked around for his hat, remembered that it was downstairs, and started toward the door. Hilary followed him, and they were alone together on the stairs.

"I shall come back this evening to see that those bandages are not too tight, Mrs.—"

But he was held back from the refuge of formality by the keenness of Hilary's gray eyes, and the amusement in them.

"You had better call me 'Hilary,' " she said, with a slight smile. "Mother prefers to have the other name forgotten. Besides, haven't I known you all my life?"

"Known me—?"

"Since the days when you used to hang on the hitching chains and watch me ride."

"You remember that?" He flushed unhappily. "I have thought of you so much since . . . but I had never supposed you noticed. . . ."

"Maidens of even such tender years are conscious enough of admiration."

"And you knew me again, after all this time?"

"Oh, I shouldn't have known your face. I knew the name when I heard it, because I had asked my brother Tom, once, what the little boy's name was who lived in the brick house on the corner of Main Street. You knew Tom?"

"Yes—I knew him, slightly." But he had not been aware of it until now.

"You see, then. We are childhood friends." The corners of her mouth drew down in a mocking smile. "You will call me Hilary, and I shall call you—Dr. Martin."

"Very well." He bowed. "No, you mustn't come down with me. I can find my way. Undress the child, and make her comfortable in bed."

They shook hands, and he went on down the stairs and into the library in search of his hat. Mrs. Baird was there, waiting for him.

"How is she? Is it a bad break?"

"Simple fracture. Never very serious, with a child. Their bones knit quickly, you know."

"She won't be lame?"

"Oh, no—not if she's properly cared for."

"And you will do that, won't you?" For the first time, she smiled at him. "You see—she is"—he saw the suppressed words trembling on her lips, "she is all I have," or "she is very dear to me," but she held them back and murmured—"she is such a nice child, if she is naughty."

"She is a very beautiful child."

"Yes, I suppose so." He saw that she admitted it reluctantly, and was not surprised.

"I shall come to see her often, if you don't mind."

"Mind? Why should I mind? On the contrary, I shall be grateful . . ." her thought raced ahead, with too few words spoken to give him more than a clue to it. "After all, I knew your aunts, once, years ago. You are the Martin Child who was raised by Miss Jenny and her sister? . . . And besides, Hilary needs someone her own age to liven her up a little. . . . Yes, and no one ever comes here except of necessity." (He wondered why, if she wanted them to come, she kept the gates locked. This must be a very sudden notion on her part.)

He shook hands with her, and she walked to the hall door with him.

"Oh, Doctor—I didn't think. You climbed the fence to get in?"

"Yes. How else?"

"Well, you won't want to come back that way. I'll give you my key to the padlock."

She took it from the hook behind the door and

gave it to him; he thanked her gravely and turned away to cross the terrace.

Oddly enough, as he walked away, disappointment was the only nameable emotion in his being. He had expected to find the women in the old Baird house queer and morbid and strange. And because he had wanted to reconcile a conception of Hilary as a morbid woman, queer and strange, with his conception of Hilary as a keen and vivid child, who did nothing without a purpose and who moved directly and uncompromisingly toward its accomplishment, he had wanted to become acquainted with her, to know her. He paused to search his mind concerning this statement that he had made to himself, and he came back to it reassured. That was why he had wanted to know her.

And he had found her not particularly strange, after all, nor had he seen any outward sign of morbidity in her mother. As a household it was no queerer than any of the completely feminine households that he knew. He thought of all the houses, dim and musty-smelling, where spinsters lived, or widows. He had been in a number of such houses in the town. The only difference was that these other women had not shut themselves away from neighborhood life. But why should Mrs. Baird not have locked her gates if she so desired? (And after all, she had made him welcome.) He did not think it strange that she had never forgiven her daughter her marriage. Her fondness for the child was perhaps odd, since she so obviously must be like her father. Lucy Anne was the whole world to her. . . . And as for Lucy Anne herself, she was too young to know that she was leading a queer unchildish sort of existence; she had no basis for comparison. And what would there have been for Hilary in the town which he had always found so vulgar—so dull? She was quite sufficient unto herself, and indifferent to the world.

Once more, he suspended his line of thought while he pondered this. He could not be quite comfortably certain that there was not something strange about Hilary, after all. He thought of her unmarred beauty. Beauty of bone, hers was, too deep in her being to depend on the color and the freshness of youth. And what woman ever cared so little for her own beauty as to be indifferent to the world? But that Hilary was not like other women did not make her morbid. Consideration of her beauty gave him no answer to his question. He went back to it. Was she somehow peculiar?

Her past had written nothing on her face except perhaps the deep lines from the curves of her nostrils to the corners of her mouth. Unless it was the shadow of the past lying in her eyes that caused the profound abstraction of her gaze. Looking at her, one felt that it was with difficulty and only for brief moments that she was able to focus on the actuality of the present. It was not abstraction, exactly, either. She gave you her attention completely, with a kind of restrained impatience at its being necessary—as if, all the time, she were anxious to return to things of more importance. But what of importance, to do or to think, was there for Hilary in that old empty house? Had she accepted her environment knowing that it need not exist for her—that she could escape from it into the past? Then indeed she had changed. . . . But it was possible that whatever it was that clouded at moments the keenness of her face was the outward and visible sign of inner concentration on some hidden and deferred intent—and not one of an idle dreaminess.

Then he remembered the fever he had felt in her fingertips when he had touched them, he remembered the flush on her cheekbones and the hollows that lay beneath them. The shadow in which she seemed to move might be the shadow of the future, and not of the past. Plain to be seen, she bore all the tokens of the plague tuberculosis.

Dr. Martin, when he reached the gate, opened it and tramped through the weeds and locked it behind him. He stepped off briskly toward his office. There would be patients waiting for him. And it was silly and futile to allow his thoughts to go maundering on in this fashion, when he would have to be going back to the Baird place for a number of weeks, and would have more than ample opportunity for observation.

2

AGAIN AND AGAIN HE RETURNED TO SEE
LUCY ANNE, AND HE HAD COME TO WON-
DER IF HILARY WERE NOT EVEN MORE
strange than he had supposed possible. He never
saw her. She was never upstairs when he was there,
nor did she appear in the library where he went
sometimes to talk with her mother. But to conclude
that she was queer because she so obviously did not
care for friendship with him was too flattering to
himself. He wondered if she could be so perverse
as to avoid him just because her mother had thought

that she needed enlivening, and had urged him to come there often.

He felt his being thwarted the more as Hilary's room, where the child still lay, seemed to promise such riches of personality in her. The room was austere in its simplicity, yet it hinted at things withheld; there was in its beauty a certain promise of inner resource in its owner which made it easy for her to dispense with decoration. Except for the heavy old mahogany furniture: the uncanopied four-poster bed, the chest of drawers and the high bureau—the room was all silver and white. The woodwork was white, and the doors, and the doorknobs were silver. The lamp on the square table beside the bed was translucent white porcelain, with a tall inverted bell of clear engraved glass around the chimney, and starred prisms hanging from it. On the mantelpiece stood a pair of silver luster vases, and on the chest of drawers, two heavy silver candlesticks. There was no color in the room, except for the few dim yellow flowers in the wall paper, the backs of the books in the open white shelves, and a grotesque piece of bright Italian pottery which stood on them, and the one old map that hung above the bed. There were no pictures on the walls, and no photographs anywhere. But the austerity of the room was softened and warmed a little by its closeness to the out-of-doors; when the door was open on to the upstairs porch, there lay beneath one's eyes a clear vista of distant fields and woods, framed by vine-covered railing and pillars. And there was always a little breeze in those vines, so that there was a continual music in the room of whispering leaves and soft summer winds.

But Dr. Martin could not build up an imaginary Hilary from his recollections of a child, his one glimpse of a woman, and his knowledge of the room that was hers. He contented himself with making friends with Lucy Anne.

As time went on he forgot that the child had once seemed to him alien. She spoke to him, and the inflections of her voice were her grandmother's and she used all her grandmother's colloquialisms; he found her a quaint little thing, and amusing, and he thought it a pity that she had no companions of her own age. His first judgment of her was that in the circumstances she was as natural a human child as possible.

And then, one morning he came unusually early to the house, and because Mrs. Baird was still busy in the kitchen, she sent him alone up to Lucy Anne. Her ankle had so far progressed by that time that she was not kept in her bed, but was carried out on the porch every morning to spend her day there, in a big chair, with her foot on a stool. When, therefore, no one answered his light knock on the bedroom door, he opened it and entered, because he assumed that she was outside and could not hear. As he had expected, he found no one in the room, but there were voices on the porch, or, rather, one voice, angry and determined. He supposed that Hilary was there, and that Lucy Anne was in some argument with her. He hesitated, therefore, on the threshold and called.

"Lucy Anne! It's the doctor. May I come in?"

He heard an embarrassed exclamation. It was followed by a pause, and then she said: "I'm out here."

He crossed to the open door, prepared to make his best bow to Hilary, but the child was alone. Except for her, the porch was empty.

"Oh! You're here all by yourself, then, and there I was all confused, thinking you had company. Who were you talking to?"

"No one. Myself." She smiled uncomfortably.

"Yourself! Oh, Lucy Anne!" He laughed at her. "It's only old, old ladies, who have no one else to talk to, who talk to themselves. And besides, you sounded so quarrelsome. Do you quarrel with yourself?"

Lucy Anne flushed a little under her olive skin. "It wasn't really with myself. It was Phoebe."

"And who is Phoebe?" Some imaginary play-mate: that was normal enough.

"Phoebe is the little girl we don't like much."

"I see. And who is 'we'?"

"Lissa. And Mary Jane. We were playing jack-stones, and Phoebe cheated."

"And you caught her, and were giving her what-for? . . . But why don't you ever have real little girls here to play with you? I should think your games with Phoebe would tire the imagination."

"But they are real little girls," she protested. "I didn't just make them up. They were grand-mother's friends when she was young." And Lucy Anne told him about the diary and the table of cousins, like the table of the kings of England, and about all the people, young and old, who had be-longed to the house, and how her grandmother had told her stories about them.

"So you see," she concluded, "I don't have to make them up. They're *here*." Then, impressed by his baffled incredulous expression, she added: "I mean there's something of them still here. In the walls. And they come to play when I want them."

"You mean—you actually *see* them?"

Lucy Anne had grown fond of the doctor for his kindness and unwearied tenderness, but now he seemed to her suddenly stupid.

"No. I only pretend to see them, but I really *feel them*. Don't you see?"

"I'm sorry. I suppose it is dense of me. . . . How are you feeling? Do you get tired and sick of being tied to a chair?"

"Not out here, much. There's a lot to think about. Do you know you can see the steeple of the old church from here? Over there behind those trees." She pointed across the fields.

"Yes, I see. The old deserted Baptist church. Is that one of the things you think about?"

"Not the church, exactly. But the graveyard. My great-great-grandfather Richard Hewitt is buried there, and his wife. I made a song about it once. But oh—you must never tell any one that—I forgot—Grandmother doesn't like songs."

"Maybe"—he laughed again—"it's only your songs she doesn't like. Can't say that I blame her if they're about graveyards."

For a moment longer they talked together, and he examined her bandaged leg, and then went in search of Hilary. He was determined to find her this morning, because it was not for his own sake that he wanted her, but for Lucy Anne's.

Mrs. Baird met him at the foot of the stairs to talk to him about the child. When he had expressed himself favorably as to her health and progress, he asked, casually, for Hilary. The old lady sniffed.

"She's in the laundry. Heaven knows why. You'd think she hadn't seen a man for so long that the sight of a pair of trousers sends her running. She's a queer one, is Hilary. But I'll tell her you want a word with her if you'll step into the library."

He waited, standing beside the mantelpiece until he heard her step on the doorsill. She spoke as he turned, without waiting for his apologies.

"There is nothing wrong with Lucy Anne?" But her tone was unconcerned. Hilary's was not the hen-with-one-chick attitude.

"Physically, no. But, Lord! Can't you do anything about those graveyard ideas the child's head is full of? Divert her some way?"

"Why don't you speak to Mother? She has made herself responsible for Lucy Anne's mind."

"You know she hasn't a notion of what is going on in that child's head. She would divert her if she knew."

"And the corollary?"

" 'Corollary'?"

"Isn't that the right word? She doesn't know, but would do something about it if she did. I know, but do nothing."

"That's it," he admitted. "Why don't you?" He

was depressed, and spoke gloomily. To have expected the abnormal in the beginning, and to have found what seemed like everyday sanity in the house: that had deceived him. Now he felt morbidity in the atmosphere, however submerged, and wanted Lucy Anne saved from it. "I can see," he began again, "that you are not particularly maternal—"

Mrs. Baird came to the door. She said dryly: "So you have discovered that, have you?"

He turned to her, and pleaded with her to allow Lucy Anne to have some freedom of intercourse with other children.

"But she isn't lonely. You ask her, and see what she says. She doesn't like other children."

"But think how queer she will grow up—"

"She would be what you call 'queer' at any rate, I fancy," said Hilary.

"It is madness, I tell you, madness," he protested, still, to Mrs. Baird. Hilary had withdrawn to the chair beside the window. He did not look at her, even startled as he was by her next words, spoken in her quiet, unstartling voice: "Oh, it isn't Mother who is mad. She is thinking of the future. It is Lucy Anne and I who spend our time dreaming of the dead."

Dreaming of the dead. Extraordinary household!

He thought of all the old women he knew, resigned to remembering, all else gone. But here was one whose thoughts were centered on a living child, whose memories were called upon only to entertain that child. But Hilary—if Hilary were thinking of the dead, for what was she waiting? Death? No, that was not the answer. There was strength there, in some inner core of her being, a scornful strength, not to be disturbed by trivialities. Egyptian in its passivity. Egyptian—he remembered suddenly an Egyptian head he had seen in some German museum in his student days: the head of a princess, aquiline, proud and fine, thin-cheeked and scornful-lipped. It had that same air of strength that could accept all things, untroubled, while waiting.

He felt Mrs. Baird studying his face, and he roused himself from his long silence.

"I wish you would take my advice." The two of them stepped into the hall, leaving Hilary in the window. "But you will give me no satisfaction. Believe me, Mrs. Baird, I am speaking as a physician—"

"You didn't get any satisfaction out of her, did you?" Mrs. Baird indicated her daughter by an abrupt sideways jerk of her head toward the library door. "H'm—no. Of course not." She spoke more rapidly. "She's queer, I tell you. Queer as Dick's hatband. What she needs is a husband. A husband who will beat her."

"But who will be good to Lucy Anne?" He smiled grimly.

"Oh, no." She laughed and turned off her abrupt fierce statement as a joke. "One who will leave Lucy Anne with me. . . ."

Dr. Martin had not reached the terrace steps before he heard the sound of a window opened behind him. Hilary called him. He went back and stood at the edge of the flower bed under the library window. She leaned out above him, her hands on the stone sill. For a moment she said nothing. He waited.

"You have grown fond of Lucy Anne," she said at last. "Haven't you? You and Mother. Well—as has been said so often—it's a strange world."

"Strange because we are fond of Lucy Anne?"

"No. Couldn't you fill in the blank for yourself? Strange for you and Mother to be allies. But I called you back to say that I'll take your advice, and try to distract the child's mind. Give her something to think about, I mean."

"Even if you are not maternal?"

"Oh—I could be very fond of Lucy Anne myself. But it would only be putting another weapon in Mother's hand."

"You mean that in that case you could not resist your mother's designs for her?"

"Perhaps." She smiled, and pulled the window down, and waved a farewell from behind the glass. Dr. Martin stood amazed and foolish, staring after her. Were these preposterous women trying to thwart each other through the child? And whatever in the world had she meant: he and her mother were allies. Against her? And to what purpose? He knew that he was guiltless of any inimical intent.

He clapped his hat on his head, and with a furious rapidity walked to the gate, his feet keeping time to his thoughts. He almost wished that he could say "all mad, after all. . . ." The curious hostility between the two women was clear to him now, but still obscure were its cause and its purpose—and he knew that Hilary's purpose, at least, was perfectly sane. Her gray eyes were the sanest eyes that he had ever seen, and behind the barrier that shut him out, her thought moved with crystal clarity toward some end. And behind that barrier, she was laughing at him.

3

He did not see Lucy Anne again for several days; when he made his next visit, it was on a rainy morning when he knew that the little porch would be too wet for her. Mrs. Baird went upstairs with him. Lucy Anne was in bed, lying back on the pillow; her heavy hair was unbraided and lay smooth and heavy and black over her shoulders.

"Hello," he said. "What a monstrous lot of hair. Like Rapunzel."

"It's the wrong color. Don't you remember: 'Let down your golden hair'?"

"Perhaps it isn't Rapunzel, then. Perhaps it is the Sleeping Beauty."

"Perhaps it is." She surveyed him gravely. "Then you must be the Prince. Then when my ankle is well and I can get up, you must kiss me, and it will be like waking after a thousand years."

"Don't be silly." Her grandmother picked up a hairbrush and approached the bed. "Let me braid your hair and make you tidy for the doctor."

"Mother said I could let it down. She thought it was chilly this morning, and I ought to have a dressing-jacket on, and I said my hair would keep my shoulders warm."

"Where is your mother? I thought she was up here with you?"

"She has been, all morning." Lucy Anne was emphatic, triumphant. "She just went out on the porch."

(Out in the rain, to avoid him, Dr. Martin thought.)

"We've been having a geography lesson," Lucy Anne added.

"What for? Haven't I taught you geography?"

"Not all of it. You see, I asked her what that was"—Lucy Anne pointed to the map on the wall.

Hilary had come in from the porch, and was standing behind them.

"Apparently, Mother, she had never seen a map of Italy before. So I concluded that her geography lessons had been sadly neglected."

Dr. Martin saw the furious quick glance that Mrs. Baird cast over her shoulder at Hilary.

"That map! No wonder she didn't recognize it. It's no more like Italy than—than the North Pole."

"But she knew nothing about the country. Did you, Lucy Anne?" Hilary came between them, and sat down on the edge of the bed. There was something provocative and defiant in the smiling face that she turned to her mother.

"She did not know that Florence is the most enchanting city in the world. She did not know that Columbus came from Genoa to discover America, nor that Rome is built on seven hills. She did not know," Hilary added softly, "that she was born in a little hill town near San Gimignano. San Gimignano, the town of 'a forest of towers.'"

Mrs. Baird opened her mouth, looked at Dr. Martin, and closed it again. He could see her hands quiver as she fumbled with her apron strings. She turned her back on them and walked over to the open porch door, where the rain was spattering on the sill.

"But the towers are not beautiful," Hilary continued, speaking now in the doctor's direction.

"They are rather grim and dreadful, like factory chimneys. But all the streets are cobblestones, and go twisting up and down over the old hills—"

"Hilary!" Her mother turned and came back to them. "Such talk—I forbid you—"

"Forbid?" Hilary raised her eyebrows coolly. "I am keeping to the letter of our bond—"

"Well, I'll not stay to hear you putting ideas in the child's head—"

She went out of the room and closed the door sharply behind her. Hilary looked at Dr. Martin, smiling like a mischievous child. "It was what you wanted me to do, wasn't it? Put ideas into her head?"

"Mother"—Lucy Anne propped herself up on one elbow—"do go on about the house—"

Her hair fell over her face, and she thrust it back on one side behind her ear, so that she looked like Whistler's "Little Rose of Capri."

"She was telling me about the house where I was born," she explained to the doctor. "Won't you bring a chair and sit down? Then maybe she will go on."

Dr. Martin pulled a chair to the bedside.

"I wish you would," he murmured, politely.

"Very well." Hilary drew up one knee and clasped her hands about it. She cocked her head on

139

one side and mocked him with a little twist of her mouth. "All in the cause of distraction. It was an old, old house, hundreds of years old. Perhaps it was there when Columbus left Genoa. (And perhaps it wasn't. I think it was sixteenth century, really.) It stood directly on the street—one of those cobblestone streets. And the clack of the sabots of the peasants, on the stones, when they left for the vineyards and the olive groves in the mornings— they woke you early. Across the street there lived a family of them, with a donkey, and if the sabots didn't wake you, the donkey did.

"But we never used the rooms in front, much. The salon, and the dining room. The music room was on the other side of the house, and we ate outdoors, mostly. If you came in the front door you crossed the tiled hallway to the garden door and went right out again into the court, and through the court into the garden. The house stood on what had been a hill. The lane beside us—and it was cobble-stoned, too—dropped down like a stone to the river. But the garden had been terraced: it was in two levels. And there was a wall around the upper level, and grapes grew on it. There was a fig tree there, and on one side a wall fountain with goldfish in it. There was a thatched garden house where we had tea every afternoon. The wall at the end of the upper level was only two feet high, or thereabouts, and from it a flight of stone steps led down to the lower garden, twenty feet or so below. It had flower beds and vegetables that old 'Tonio grew for us. A gate at the bottom opened into the cobblestoned lane. But we never went down there. We sat in chairs beside the low stone wall and put our feet on it, and spent the afternoons looking across the lower garden, and the red tiled roofs of the village that were still lower than the lowest garden wall, and across the tops of the Lombardy poplars that grew beside the river, and turned silver when the wind blew them one way, and green when the breeze came back. We looked over them all at the hill beyond, because on top of the hill there was a castle—an old, old, old castle, all grim and gray and warlike and forbidding. And in the bright air there were no blurred details—it was all sharp and clear and incisive, like the page of an illuminated manuscript. . . ."

Hilary talked on and on, until Dr. Martin could see it all. He was stirred more than she could know. A kind of dull resentment was making him miserable. He could not understand why he should feel that way—wistful, like a small boy who stands with face pressed against a locked gate whose key had been lost. And strangely, he kept seeing, more clearly even than the pictures she painted for them, the Italian, her husband. In the garden with her, his feet on the stone wall.

When he could endure no more, he rose to go. He had not once that morning been the physician-in-attendance, but he saw that Lucy Anne had no need of him. He shook hands stiffly with Hilary, and congratulated her on her success in distracting the child's mind. She wondered why he looked flushed and angry. Once more, at the hall door, he found Mrs. Baird waiting for him. She was both querulous and curious.

"Hilary, I suppose, is still talking about Italy. I wish she wouldn't, it's so unsettling. Did she seem interested?"

"Lucy Anne? Yes, entranced."

"And now she'll be thinking about heaven knows what."

"But surely it won't do the child any harm to think about Italy?"

"Yes, it will." He was taken aback at the determined and obstinate expression on her face. Her mouth had straightened into a set, tight line. "Just unsettle her mind for nothing. Nothing, I tell you."

He wanted to laugh and pat the old lady reassuringly on the shoulder and say "all right, all right," but what he did say was "You think then, that she will want to go—to see Italy?"

"Hilary," the old lady snapped, "Hilary wants to go. But she needn't think she can get at me that way. I simply will not have it. I do wish," and the querulousness in her voice became more pronounced, "I do wish she would marry in this country, some decent man, and settle down. Then I could wash my hands of her."

For the first time Dr. Martin that morning wondered if he were not in love with Hilary. That hot emotion which had so disturbed him while he listened to her description of the house above the valley of the Elsa: could it be anything but jealousy? And if he were jealous of a man long since dead, must it not be because he loved his widow?

Hilary. The beauty of the name that his mind dwelt on brought to the eye of his imagination the beauty of the woman, and for a moment he was happy because he had been with her but now, and would be with her again on the morrow.

If he loved her now, he must have loved her always. He was moved by the thought of his patient and enduring love. . . . But how could he be sure? Perhaps because he had, for so long a while, remembered the beautiful child, he had unconsciously determined to love the woman, whenever he might come to know her. Suppose you said to yourself, there is a woman whom it would be good to love. When you found yourself, thereafter, in love with her, would it be love? How could you know?

And then he smiled at himself, disdainful of his uncertain mind. *Hilary.* . . .

Two weeks had passed since Lucy Anne's accident. Dr. Martin removed the splints from her ankle, and put on a plaster-of-Paris bandage. He promised to bring her soon a pair of crutches, so that she could move about upstairs without being carried. In the meantime, she told him, she was playing a new game. The porch railing was a low stone wall. She could put her feet on it and look out over the Lombardy poplars that lined a river bank, and beyond the trees stood a hill, and on the hill a castle. And she sat there beside the wall, with a fig tree and a wall fountain full of goldfish behind her, and looked at the castle and thought of all the things that had happened within its gates. And then again, sometimes the porch was the deck of an ocean steamer, and the railing a ship's railing, and there was nothing to be seen except waves, blue or green or gray, edged with white, moving past swiftly, once in a while bearing with them a whale or an iceberg or another ship.

Dr. Martin joined in these games. One morning he stood leaning over the railing—a ship's railing—and told her how the waters, held away from the ship in a solid slanting wall by the terrible force of its going, looked like green marble veined with white. He heard Lucy Anne, behind him, interrupt his monologue with the murmur "You see, we're on a ship. . . ." He turned and saw Hilary in the door. She no longer avoided him, and he had come to expect her to appear like this suddenly, silently without a word.

"We are on our way—to Italy, I suppose?" He turned to Lucy Anne. She nodded her head eagerly.

"Why?" Hilary wanted to know.

"Why not? You want to go there, do you not?"

"Now? This very day? Not particularly," she said indifferently. "Why?"

"Your mother seems to think that it is an obsession of yours."

"Italy for Italy's sake? What nonsense! Mother knows better than that. One place is very much like another place, except for the people that are in it."

"I see." Jealousy and hopelessness and understanding were confused in him. "Your friends are there?" He wished he did not feel with such damnable clearness how dull and ordinary he must seem to her.

"My friends? No, I have no friends there, except possibly the nuns who taught where I went to school."

He understood, and was relieved. It was for Lucy Anne's sake that she wanted to go. Perhaps she thought the child should know her father's people. But that was too small a thing for Hilary to be so intent upon. Hilary, made for high ends. He was disappointed. It was sad how a life could become so hemmed in by trivialities, like clear swift streams that in the end lost themselves muddily in beds of cattails and watercress. But he wanted Hilary for himself—and could he make himself believe that he was the high end for which she had been created? Hardly! He returned with a kind of violent abruptness to the conversation. Lucy Anne had been telling her mother about the green sea waves and an iceberg on the horizon. . . .

Dr. Martin said that when he came again he would bring the crutches, and that when she tried to walk with them, she could pretend that she was trying to walk on a sloping deck in a rough sea. He said good-bye to Hilary and made his way downstairs.

Mrs. Baird had not lately interrupted his visits

with Hilary and Lucy Anne, but she always stood waiting for him in the hall when he came away. She was there that day, looking up the stairs as he came down. He explained to her about the plaster-of-Paris bandages and the crutches.

"She will soon be about again," he said cheerfully.

"I suppose you won't be coming back afterwards, to see us? Hilary will miss you. . . ."

"Hilary?"

"She likes you so much," her mother murmured, a little embarrassed by the amusement in his face.

"Look here," he said, "you're not trying the Beatrice and Benedick dodge on us, are you?"

She showed no recognition of the allusion.

"I was only going to say how glad I am to see her showing interest in anyone."

"Please," he interrupted her, "don't say again that you hope she will marry. Surely you can see"— he hesitated—"that she isn't very well—"

"I can see that she looks like she was going off in a galloping consumption. But she isn't, because she's looked that way for weeks—months. Besides, it can be cured nowadays, can't it?"

"If taken in time—perhaps," he admitted, cautiously.

"You should examine her."

147

"I hardly need to. She should go west at once."

"Well, then—speak to her about it."

He looked at the old woman rather grimly. "You would let her go?"

"Certainly, and pay her way. Lucy Anne," she added, "could stay here with me. There is danger of infection, isn't there?" He knew that she was glad that there was danger of infection.

"But what if it is too late for such a cure? Some provision should be made for the child—"

"You need not worry about Lucy Anne," she said, and with that he was sufficiently rebuked for not having minded his own business, but she added, gratuitously, "she is mine until I die, and afterwards—I have made my will." Her mouth straightened into the set stubborn line that he found so disconcerting. "If my children want my money, Lucy Anne will go to her Uncle Tom to be brought up with his daughter. I don't like Hilary's—ideas. Lucy Anne should have a normal young person's life. If they keep the conditions of my will, at twenty-one she shall have this house and land."

He was intensely, but very quietly, angry at the insult to Hilary. That she had never seemed to care for the child made no difference.

"You surely don't think," he said, "that she has been leading a normal life here?"

"What do you mean?"

"No solitary child is normal. Lucy Anne has some morbid streaks in her. I told you before—the child should be in school with other children."

"Here, with all the rag-tag and bobtail in town?"

"Here, or elsewhere. There are schools that are—er—superior to the rag-tag—"

"Send her away from here? No, indeed." She shook her head. "Not while I am alive. I want her roots to go so deep here that she can't get them up again, completely."

Dr. Martin thought of Lucy Anne upstairs on the deck of her ocean liner, and smiled. . . . But afterwards, he wondered why he had smiled, in that superior fashion. For he had understood that to Lucy Anne there had been reality in the games with Melissa and Phoebe and the rest of them. The castle across the river, the sloping boat deck—these were only make-believe. He thought that the child had taken root, and that it was foolish of Hilary to be so determined to transplant her. Lucy Anne had as great a chance for happiness here as anywhere. The Baird house and the Baird land would be no contemptible inheritance.

4

THE SUMMER DAYS PASSED QUICKLY; AUGUST CAME TO AN END. LUCY ANNE, ON HER CRUTCHES, WAS NO LONGER CONfined upstairs, but hobbled all over the house. Dr. Martin still came to see her, and to see Hilary. He no longer questioned the reality of his love for her. He had awakened in the middle of one night, knowing. If she would marry him, he had said to himself, he would give up his practice here and take her to New Mexico or Arizona, where she could be cured. And if a man were willing to break his life in two for a woman, unhesitatingly, then he loved her.

He told her one day that he was afraid that she had tuberculosis. She was indifferent, neither shocked nor surprised, and refused to allow him to examine her.

"It is as easy a way to die as another," she said.

He scolded her vehemently, but to no avail. She came to the door with him as he was going, and he turned back from the step and asked her to walk to the gate with him.

"I don't think that I have finished all that I want to say."

She laughed, as at an importunate, troublesome child, and came outside and walked with him, her sandals noiseless on the grass-grown drive.

"You might at least take to gardening," he said, after a moment's pause.

"I have hardened my heart. And who knows but it might be softened by the feeling of soil between my fingers?"

"You are fighting it, then—all this?" He moved his free hand, to indicate the maple trees, the deep shadows on the grass, the tawny, seeded grass—green and gold and tawny. Her eyes did not follow his gesture, but remained level and unseeing.

"Not fighting, no. I haven't seen it—not since I was a child."

"Look, then. Life for you may lie in your seeing it as you did—"

"It is the same, then, and only I have changed?" She smiled a little, sardonically, as she looked from the tall grass to the black branches of trees, and back into his face. "But surely you can see that life does not matter much to me. Except"—her mouth tightened grimly—"I must outlive Mother."

"Then," he said brusquely, shocked a little, "I advise you to cultivate your garden."

"It is as bad as that? Or are you taking refuge in your brutality from mine? . . . You do not understand, and I do not know why it is important to me that you should. But can't you see that the way to damnation for me lies in my allowing her to have her way with Lucy Anne? If I were to die first, or if I let this"—now her gesture indicated their surroundings—"come to have any meaning for me—"

"If you die before your mother, then Lucy Anne would inherit all this—and she loves it. Why not?"

"She would grow up here," her smile was frankly mocking now. "And sometime bring a husband here, and have children, and the old days would come again. That is what you think? And why not?"

"Yes. Why not?" He spoke almost indifferently, but he held his breath. He would learn now the source of combat between those strange self-contained women.

"Her birthright for a mess of pottage. She is her father's daughter, and a musician born."

"I see." And he did see. More clearly than if she had bared to him her inmost mind. Hilary Baird was still thinking of her husband, after all these years, and lest something should lessen the intensity of that thought, she had closed her mind, and, as she had said, hardened her heart. Lucy Anne's happiness—that did not weigh the balance in the slightest. She was to be a musician. . . . He straightened himself, sighed, and returned to what he had thought of saying, a moment ago.

"But even if your mother dies first, you know, Lucy Anne is to go to your brother Tom." He saw by her face that she did not know, but it was too late. "By the terms of your mother's will. I'm sorry—I did not know that I was betraying a confidence, she spoke so frankly of it to me."

"I am glad you told me. She must be persuaded to change her will—or I shall be forced to defy it."

"Then, if you do want to live"—he became once more bland and kind—professional—"you must fight for it."

"I shall take to planting—pansies and forget-me-nots—in the garden, and think of something else at the same time. It is a game in which I have had practice."

He unlocked the gate, and she gave him her hand in good-bye.

He had not had the courage, after all, to ask her to marry him, nor to say that he would take her to New Mexico or Arizona. But not until Lucy Anne was ready to throw away the crutches would he have to return the key to the padlock on the gate. On that day he would speak.

The day came, for him, all too quickly. He told Lucy Anne good-bye, and tucked the crutches under his arm; he told Mrs. Baird good-bye, and said that if Lucy Anne limped unduly, or had trouble with her ankle, to bring her to his office for electrical massage. He asked for Hilary, and was told that she was out of doors. He went out, the crutches still under his arm, in search of her. He was embarrassed and a little self-conscious, because he had felt Lucy Anne wanting to go with him, and her grandmother holding her back.

He found Hilary transplanting the foxgloves under the library window. She held up her grimed hands, palms outward.

"You see, I am amenable to advice. At least"— she stopped the words in his mouth—"in so far. You have not come with more, have you?"

"Not advice. Argument. No, not even argument. Pleading."

"In whose cause? Lucy Anne's?"

"Yes, and your own. Tell me the truth, now, Hilary, will you? . . . You refuse to admit anything into your mind but the idea of taking Lucy Anne back to Italy. But why? She would have no greater chance for happiness there, and you may not succeed. And in the meantime—"

"In the meantime?"

"You are having no life at all, only an existence. Are you never tempted from your purpose?"

"Sometimes, lately. I am very tired." She faced him frankly. Candor sat upon her brow, but her mouth was set, and the lines from nostril to lip deepened until they showed themselves harsh and weary. "Often I am tempted to give myself up to my daily life. Little things make for content, if you let them. Is that what you mean?"

"Not exactly. I mean, don't you ever wish that you had what other women have? A home—" He was betrayed into the banality. "A woman's normal life?"

"But—'a woman's normal life'—here?" She was able to smile a little as she bent her head sideways toward the house wall.

"Oh, not here—"

"Yes?"

"I meant marriage." He flushed uneasily.

"Marriage! Again? Impossible! So you and Mother. . . . But who—?" Then her eyes widened, softened. She turned white. "You mean yourself? Oh, no!" She shook her head slowly. "Even if I could, I would not."

"Why? Hilary, listen, please—" He felt more confident now, less remote. Her very amazement roused his combativeness, lessened his sense of the preposterous. Besides, the sight of her, looking so slight, so ill, stirred in him an infinite tenderness, and tenderness and awe are incompatible emotions. With her pallid cheek, and her body trembling until her teeth chattered, she no longer seemed to him withdrawn and unassailable. "I told you, Hilary," he continued gently, "how I had never forgotten you—you and the pony, when we were children—"

She continued to shake her head slowly, her jaws tightly locked to stop her teeth chattering, but he did not heed.

"You will not believe me, but I was as bitterly unhappy when I heard of your marriage as if—as if I had had some right to be. You have always been in my heart—" He stumbled over the inept phraseology.

"No." She could laugh, now. She could always

laugh at what sounded sentimental. "Not in your heart. In your imagination. Think, Dr. Martin. Isn't it your imagination that has been busy with me all this time?"

"No, I love you." He stood his ground stubbornly. "And Lucy Anne, too."

"And in about the same way, I think. We are like nothing in your world, and therefore appeal to your imagination. You think you desire to bring us into it."

"I do. I think I could make my world over for you. I should take you to New Mexico to live, where you would be strong again—"

"You would do that?—but you mustn't say anything more. I am sorry to have been so startled. Of course it was not because it is inconceivable to think of loving you—" Once more she smiled easily and frankly at him. "That would be too silly. It is because—I thought you must have seen"—the words came slowly, as if they were being forced out of her, yet she spoke with a kind of matter-of-fact simplicity—"that I live with Paolo—in my mind—day and night. He is the background of my life. And so of course—" She shrugged her shoulders.

"Then you are never tempted to forget him?"

"Never." She dropped her eyes, but answered without hesitation. "I couldn't."

"I see. Then I had better not come back again?"

"You had better forget us. Until we need you again. I am selfish enough to insist that, as a physician, you should be at our beck and call."

"Very well. And you will take care of yourself?"

"The best of care. Milk and eggs, and sleep on the porch, and all the rest of it."

"And don't overtire yourself."

"It is unlikely. I am bone-lazy."

"Good. . . . Tell Aaron, will you, that I shall leave the key in the padlock when I have locked the gate behind me? . . . And good-bye—for this time—"

Dr. Martin walked alone down the driveway. He wondered when he would see her again. He thought that he had not asked her for the last time to marry him. He would some day come upon her in a moment of despair, when she would have foreseen defeat . . . and she would have been thinking of his love, and it would not seem so impossible to her to accept it. But if then she should in desperation consent to marry him, he would know that she was not the Hilary whom he had perhaps, after all, created.

IV

1

WHEN DR. MARTIN HAD SAID GOOD-
BYE TO HER FOR THE LAST TIME, AND
HAD GONE, AND THE GATE HAD BEEN
locked behind him, it seemed to Lucy Anne as if he
had never been there, as if the last weeks had been
a dream. Now her mother spoke to her no more of
Italy, and her grandmother once more superin-
tended her lessons. There was only one thing different, and that was the way in which her grandmother
watched her mother, as if she were waiting for her
to say something important. But Hilary said noth-

ing, and Mrs. Baird was constrained to go on with
her daily life as if she had expected no change in it.

As soon as Lucy Anne was able to walk about
beneath the maple trees, whose leaves, now, were
beginning to fall, dry and yellow, beneath the September sun, Mrs. Baird began to make her plans for
a day with her son Tom in the neighboring city.
Annually she made this brief visit, "spent the day"
with them; annually she laid plans for it days ahead
of time, giving it some momentous quality, as the
only break in the monotony of her life in the old
house. Annually she went off alone, early one morning, leaving Hilary and Lucy Anne together in the
house, and returned alone late at night.

Hilary had been waiting, since Dr. Martin's reve-
lations, for some mention by her mother of this
visit. It came one afternoon when the old lady and
the little girl had finished an hour of spelling-and-
reading, and had settled down to their recreation.
Mrs. Baird was adding up her accounts; Lucy Anne,
on the floor, was cutting out paper dolls.

"I think that on Saturday I'll go over to Tom's.
Haven't been, yet, this summer. I shouldn't want
them to think. . . ." Her voice trailed off; she was
talking more to herself than to the others.

Hilary did not speak at once of what was in her
mind; she waited for half an hour, to give to her

suggestion some semblance of suddenness, as if it had just occurred to her. Then she said, slowly, "You know, Mother, I think Dr. Martin was right about Lucy Anne. She should have some companionship with children her own age. She is getting to be a little old lady before her time."

Both Lucy Anne and her grandmother looked up, the one startled and hopeful, the other startled and hostile.

"What do you mean?" Mrs. Baird demanded. "You wouldn't put her in school here with all the ragamuffins in this town?"

"No, I shouldn't."

"H'm. It's just as well, because I would not hear of it. What do you suggest, then? Not inviting children here, I hope, to go home and tell their gaping mothers tales about how we live?"

"No, not that, either. It merely occurred to me that since you are going to Tom's, you might take Lucy Anne with you. Tom's Margaret can't be more than a year or two older than Lucy Anne, and surely there's no harm in the child's making friends with her own first cousin?"

Lucy Anne had scrambled to her feet, scattering snips of paper and paper dolls broadcast, and had gone to stand beside her grandmother's knee. Mrs.

Baird did not look at her, but surveyed doubtfully her impassive and indifferent daughter.

"No, there would be no harm. In fact, I think it's a very good idea, but considering the way you've always sneered at Tom, I'm surprised—"

"Not Tom. Tom's wife. But no doubt his daughter takes after the Bairds." There was an ironic gleam in her eye. Her mother, a little uncomfortable, turned to Lucy Anne, who had listened silently and breathlessly.

"Would you like to go with me on Saturday to spend the day with your Cousin Margaret?"

The child nodded her head. Her heart leaped tumultuously beneath the ruffles of her pinafore. She was afraid to speak, lest by speaking she spoil it.

"Very well. I'll write to Tom at once, and have Aaron mail it."

Lucy Anne waited until the note was written and irrevocably gone, then she turned to her mother.

"Won't you go, Mother?"

"No, not I." Hilary grimaced. "Someone has to stay home and see that Aaron doesn't get into mischief."

Before Saturday, Mrs. Baird went into the town one morning and came back with an armful of hats and slippers for Lucy Anne to try on. She chose a white hat with a limp wide brim, and streamers down the back, and the only pair of slippers large enough, and Aaron was sent to return all the others.

If it had not been for the hat, Lucy Anne would have felt quite sick on Saturday morning, when Aaron unlocked the gate, and she emerged into the town with her grandmother, clinging to her hand. But the hat was one that you could hide under: you had only to hang your head, and no one could see under the wide brim. People might be staring at you, but you were spared the knowledge of it.

The faint threat of sickness that gathered like a lump beneath the end of her breastbone made Lucy Anne brief of speech, curt in her responses to her grandmother's flurried essays at conversation, but she kept tight hold of her hand while they rounded the court house, crossed the main street, and mounted the high steps into the monstrous interurban car that stood there waiting.

Once in a seat, next to the window, Lucy Anne dropped her grandmother's hand and peered down curiously at the stragglers on the sunny corner. But she was quite unprepared for the clamor that rose and assaulted her ears when the car was started. The wheels shrieked and squeaked on the rails as they swung around the corner, the electricity spluttered and crackled, and something under the floor was let loose in a kind of roaring hum. The sickness in Lucy Anne's breast rose and enveloped her; she turned a white and terrified face to her grandmother.

"Gran," she implored, "what *is* it? Is it always like this, or is something wrong?"

Her grandmother laughed, and took her hand again.

"The noise, you mean? Oh, it's always like this. You look out of the window, and you'll forget it in a minute."

Lucy Anne turned to the window, but her eyes were tight shut; she sat and waited to be hurled to destruction. But nothing happened. She opened her eyes, and saw that they were already in the country. They swooped down hills and around curves at an appalling rate. Something terrible was bound to happen. The car swayed from side to side; the steady roaring hum increased in volume.

Outside the window there were cornfields: unlimited cornfields. You could hardly see where they ended, except that there were trees there, along the edges. The cornstalks beside the tracks went past in a blur that it made you dizzy to watch. It was safer to watch the trees. The farther away they were, the longer you could see them. Lucy Anne sought the most distant, held it until it was gone, sought ahead again, another most distant. Gradually her terror and sickness subsided.

The car stopped. It was all alone in the midst of the cornfields. There was a sudden uprush of silence. People stirred a little uneasily in their seats, and spoke in subdued voices. The sun centered upon the car, like a palpable weight, and there was no shelter from it anywhere, as far as eye could see, except beneath one of the scattered, scraggly trees. You could hear flies, buzzing. The heat and the flies and the whispers, that had been blown away in the wind of their going, had fallen upon them again in this awful pause.

"Gran," Lucy Anne murmured, "what's the matter now?"

"Matter? Nothing's the matter." Her grandmother's voice was so loud in the hushed silence that Lucy Anne in discomfiture hid again beneath her hat. "We're waiting here on the switch for the car going the other way, that's all. Watch for it, there on your side."

Lucy Anne watched, but it came so suddenly, like a thunderbolt, with such a roar and so close to her very nose, that she drew back with a little cry of dismay. But their own car had started, and no one had heard her in the clatter. She blushed undetected.

Not long after that the cornfields began to give way to scattered rows of houses, set like cardboard boxes on the scarred, grassless fields. They seemed to Lucy Anne too tiny to be real, too new for people really to live in. And they clustered thicker and thicker together as the car proceeded, until the fields were gone. There were no trees, either, only sick-looking saplings set in front of the rows of brightly painted boxes. Lucy Anne tried to count the people that must live along here where the car passed, supposing that there were three in each house. But they passed too quickly. She became depressed at the thought of so many, many people living packed tight together like this. Once more she turned to her grandmother.

"How much longer, now?"

"Oh—quite a little while till we get right down into the city. Then we have to take another car to Greenvale Street."

Greenvale Street sounded rather like maple trees and lots of grass. Lucy Anne remembered her great anticipations of this day, and began to be happier. At the end of this trip there would be a little girl to play with.

Once in the city streets, with turmoil rising on all sides of the car, she lost all power to collect definite impressions. Her head whirled, she was in a daze at finding herself in the center of so much confusion. At last the car stopped dead, and everyone rose and made for the doors. She followed her grandmother, and her knees trembled as she walked down the steps. Even her grandmother was flurried and uncertain; she had to ask someone which car to take to Greenvale Street. And then they had to cross the street and stand for a long while on the curb while things whirled past them. At last the right car came along, and they went out into the street and climbed its steps. Lucy Anne breathed more easily, even although it meant that the noises would begin again.

But this second car was smaller than the first one, and did not go so fast. It bumped and rattled more—all the windows were loose and rattled—but it did not roar, nor sway from side to side. Mrs. Baird asked the conductor to tell them when they reached Greenvale Street. They stopped at almost every corner, and every time Lucy Anne looked for the conductor; when he happened to catch her eye, he would smile and shake his head, and she would settle back in her seat reassured. It was not until she had resigned herself to going on and on forever that he finally called out, in a loud voice that made them jump, "Greenvale Street." They rose and scuttled for the door, as if they might not be allowed time to get off. When they stood at last in the street, a bell in the car tink-tinkled, and it went on down the tracks and left them there alone.

Lucy Anne looked in vain for grass and maple trees. It was a street just like all they had passed, of mean little houses set close together. Only here, they were not so brightly painted, and the few sycamore trees along the curb had outgrown the sapling stage.

"But Grandmother," she remonstrated, "this can't be it."

"Oh, yes, it is. I know the street well enough once I reach it. But what an awful jaunt!" She sighed, and straightened her hat and Lucy Anne's. "There you are! I guess we'll do. Your Uncle Tom lives in the third house beyond the second cross street."

Soon Lucy Anne could see that her Uncle Tom's house had a little porch on it, and that there were two little girls there, in a swing. One of them, of course, would be her cousin, Margaret Baird. Her hold on her grandmother's hand tightened.

When they were in front of the first house beyond the cross street, one of the little girls slipped out of the swing and stepped to the door.

"Hey, Mom! Here they are!"

Then she turned, ran down the porch steps and

embraced her grandmother with a kind of sticky fervor that knocked her hat awry.

"Hello, Grandmother Baird—it's a month of Sundays since we've seen you." She pretended not to notice Lucy Anne until she was introduced to her.

"This is your cousin Lucy Anne, Margaret. We thought it was high time you were getting acquainted."

"Sure is," Margaret agreed affably, and shook Lucy Anne's limp hand. They went up the steps together. Behind the screen door stood a short fat woman in a white dress. Her face was red and her hair unkempt and frizzled. Hers was a louder heartiness even than her daughter Margaret's.

"Well, Mother Baird, I do declare! It's high time you were lookin' in on us. Come in and drop your hats. So this is little Lucy Anne!" She kissed Lucy Anne gingerly on the cheek. "I must say she don't take after Hilary a little bit in looks." Lucy Anne stared at her a moment, then withdrew her gaze and stood awkwardly, her hands clasped behind her back. She heard a whisper. ". . . Bashful? She'll get over it with Margaret. There's nothing bashful about her. . . ." Then the louder tones, addressed to her, "You will want to play with Margaret and her little friend Eileen, won't you? They know all kinds of games. You take her, Margaret, and play out on the porch."

Margaret seized her elbow, but Lucy Anne waited to see what her grandmother was going to do. The old lady had hung her hat up on the rack, and laid her purse on the seat beneath it, and now she made a motion to sit down on one of the knobby yellow rocking chairs.

"Now, Mother Baird, don't drop into the first chair you see. You're tryin' to make me think it's an awful journey over here. You can't fool me that way. You know you could manage to come oftener if you wanted to." This was said with a heavy archness, a kind of false geniality. "No, come along upstairs, where there's an electric fan, and we can get a little breeze through the windows. This sittin' room is just too awful in hot weather." The stairs rose directly from the end of the room, and they had started up them, old Mrs. Baird in front. "But poor dear Tom just can't afford a bigger house just now." At her conclusion she shot a venomous glance at her mother-in-law's unconscious back. Lucy Anne shivered with repugnance, and wondered if her grandmother really liked Aunt Eleanore. Probably not, she thought, or she would come oftener.

She followed Margaret to the door. She would be glad not to have to stay in the close, sour-smelling little sitting room. . . . Margaret, she noticed, was quite a little larger than she. Her hair was short and light, her face broad and freckled, her mouth wide.

"Come along, kid," she said. "We ain't gonna bite you. 'T least, I ain't seen Eileen bite anybody yet," she added facetiously. "This is Eileen Monaghan, an' she lives down the street apiece. An' this is my kid cousin, from the country." She made a little grimace which Lucy Anne saw out of the corner of her eye. Her heart sank. She seated herself stiffly in the swing beside the green-eyed, auburn-haired Eileen.

"What'll we play? Come on, now, Eileen. You gotta help me entertain my guest." There was a sarcastic emphasis on the last word. It was not lost on Lucy Anne.

"I don't have to be entertained," she said, coolly. "I am able to take care of myself."

"It's too hot for games, anyway, Peg," Eileen intervened. "Let's just set an' talk." She had a large blonde doll lying in her lap, and was engaged in smoothing its organdy ruffles.

"Is that your doll?" Lucy Anne asked her, politely. "Isn't she e-*nor*-mous!"

"It's Peg's. She is big, ain't she. I tell you, Peg. Let's play operation. In the house, not out here. I'll be the nurse, and you be the doctor, and you"—she

173

turned and thrust the doll into Lucy Anne's arms—
"you can be her mother."

Lucy Anne felt happier with the doll in her arms.
Margaret opened the screen door, and they followed her into the house. She pulled a doll's bed
out of a cupboard, and offered Lucy Anne the rather
grimy sheets and a nightgown.

"Put her to bed, and then send for me. My office
will be in the parlor." She indicated a dark little
room beyond a half-open door, within which she
and Eileen disappeared.

Lucy Anne undressed the doll and put her to bed.
She thought of Dr. Martin, and smiled happily at
the doll. When she had tucked her in she rose and
crossed the room and knocked on the parlor door.

"Good morning, Dr. Baird," she said, gravely.
"I'm afraid my little girl is sick. Will you come and
see?"

"Is she *very* sick?"

"I—er—I don't think so."

"Well, I'd better bring the nurse along, and be on
the safe side. Nurse!"

The three of them returned to the doll's bedside.
The doctor turned to Lucy Anne.

"Madam, I must ask you to leave the room while
we make the examination."

Lucy Anne withdrew a little space and watched

them. They turned the doll's nightgown back and examined her pink wax abdomen with what seemed to the anxious mother undue levity. They whispered together and snickered.

"Madam," Margaret turned to her, "it's just as I feared. Your child must have an operation at once. We'll take her to the hospital now."

"But, doctor, may I ask what her trouble seems to be?"

They snickered again, and Lucy Anne felt her cheeks growing hot.

"That will be easier to say after we've performed the operation. Come, nurse, bring the child."

Lucy Anne followed them to the parlor door. There Eileen stopped her, a firm hand against her chest.

"You can't come in. Mothers aren't allowed at operations."

They closed the door, but Lucy Anne could still hear them giggling. She felt hot all over. She loathed them both, and she would not play their games. She turned from the door and looked about the little room, full of shiny yellow furniture and bristling with chair rockers. There was nothing to play with, and no books, except three or four behind a glass door over a desk. It was a queer desk, Lucy Anne thought: streaky yellow, like all the furniture, with brass curlicues around the keyholes, and above, half shelves for books, with a glass door, half-open shelves without a door, but with carved supports, for vases and photographs. The books were out of her reach, but on the shelf beneath the center table lay a large flat black volume.

She pulled it out and opened it. Of the printing she could read not a word: she stared at it, fascinated, but could make nothing of the strange combinations of letters. But the pictures told their own story. The austere figure of a man, robed in black and with a wreath on his head, wandered in them through strange places, watching from his rock through smoke and flame while devils with hoofs and forked tails danced about naked bodies piled grotesquely in the background. They were pictures of nightmares, Lucy Anne thought, worse than she could imagine anyone dreaming. She opened the book on the floor and lay down on her stomach above it.

Presently the parlor door opened behind her, and the two girls came out.

"Madam," said the doctor, "I have to report that your child is doing as well as could be expected."

"Oh?" said Lucy Anne, without looking up. "But I'm not playing."

"Oh, *ain't* you?" said the red-headed Eileen. "Why not?"

"I'd rather read."

Eileen came and looked over her shoulder.

"For the love o' Mike! Can you read that? It's wop writin'."

Margaret came and looked over her shoulder, too.

" 'Course she can. She is a wop, didn't you know that?"

Lucy Anne looked over her shoulder at them, flames of resentment burning in her black eyes.

"What is a wop? I'm not one, whatever it is."

"Oh, yes, you are. A dago, an Eye-talian. You can't say your father wasn't an Eye-talian, because he was."

Lucy Anne couldn't say so, because she did not know. She turned back to the book to hide the threat of tears.

"But my land, Peg!" Eileen sneered at them both. "My mother don't allow me to play with no wops. I don't care if she is your cousin. I gotta go."

"Oh, look here, Eileen!" Margaret followed her to the door. "It don't mean nothin', her bein' a wop, because she's always lived with Grandma Baird."

"I gotta go, just the same. So long, Peg."

"You mean you wantta go. Well, s'long."

Two fugitive tears ran down Lucy Anne's cheeks. She turned the page hastily—two pages, to hide the blisters the tears had made in falling. And to think she had wanted to come here. . . . It was because her father had been an Italian, then, that people wouldn't play with her . . . but if they were like Eileen and Margaret, she didn't want to play with them. . . .

"Look here, kid, put the ol' book up, an' we'll play something. Know how to play Parcheesi?"

"No."

"Well, there ain't nothin' to it. I'll soon show you."

When old Mrs. Baird and her daughter-in-law came downstairs to get lunch, their eyes were met by the comfortable sight of two little girls squatting over the Parcheesi board. Lucy Anne's long plaits hung over her shoulders. Margaret's short fair hair fell forward across her cheeks. They were chattering together amiably as they rattled the dice. Lucy Anne had swallowed her resentment along with her tears, and by the time her Uncle Tom came home at noon, she was quite prepared to like him.

Margaret had been listening for the noon whistles, and ran to meet him when it was time, and came back hanging on his hand. Lucy Anne waited behind the screen door.

"Hello, kid," he said, and stooped to kiss her. "It's about time you were calling on your relatives. I was beginning to think Hilary believed we weren't fit to have sight of you. You don't look much like her, do you?"

"Everyone says I don't." She flushed uneasily. "But it was Mother who asked Gran to bring me over today."

" 'Twas, eh?" He surveyed her in astonishment. "Well, Hilary always has her reasons, even if nobody knows what they are. Queerest girl for a sister a man ever had." He grimaced. "But there's nothing queer about us, is there, eh, Peg?" His mother had come into the room, and he greeted her with affection, and then he resumed, "I'm not even queer enough to want to talk before I've had my lunch. When do we eat?" He winked at Lucy Anne. She couldn't decide whether she liked him or not. Not so well as her Dr. Martin, certainly, but better than her Cousin Margaret or Aunt Eleanore.

Throughout the meal she sat in silent discomfort. She felt that Margaret was talking at her as she recounted to her grandmother tales of her school and her schoolmates, and their games. Her aunt and uncle were talking at her whenever they mentioned Hilary.

And it was such a strange meal. Sliced bologna and a dank cold potato salad, and sandwich stuff in a glass to spread on your bread, and a sodden gelatinous pie.

"You see," her Uncle Tom said once, halfway through the meal, to his mother, "what a convenience it is to have a delicatessen just around the corner."

"If you don't like it," his wife snapped at him, "you don't have to eat it. When you hire me a cook you can have the heavy hot meals you like, and not before. Catch me spending hours in the kitchen on a day like this."

It was not until the end of the meal that anyone spoke directly to Lucy Anne, except to offer her food.

"Well, young lady," her uncle said, "how would you like to spend the afternoon? How about a trip to Riverside Park?"

"What's Riverside Park?"

"There! I bet the kid's never been to an amusement park in her life."

"She hasn't," said her grandmother, "and I'm not sure I want her to go."

"Oh, Lord, Mother! Let the kid have a taste of life

while she's young. We'll all go. You can manage, can't you, Eleanore?''

''Sure. We'll just dump all this bologna and salad and bread and butter in a basket for our supper. We can buy ice cream and whatever else we want when the time comes.''

''Oh, goody!'' Margaret rose and tossed her napkin on the table. ''Can I ask Eileen, Dad?''

''I guess so. The more the merrier, eh, Lucy Anne?''

Lucy Anne wasn't so sure. Her heart sank. And there was the street car to be endured again. . . . But when the others were ready, and Eileen had been called in, she put on her hat without a word.

The street car, when there were so many of them, all together, and her uncle knew exactly where they were going, proved to be not so bad, after all. Perhaps the amusement park would be fun.

They alighted with a crowd of others before a large white gate that said ''Riverside Park'' above it in huge black letters. Uncle Tom bought tickets and they filed one by one through a turnstile, and walked down a long boardwalk in the midst of a stream of people.

There was so much noise that for a while Lucy Anne was dismayed and confused. Voices talking, high and shrill. Voices shrieking, higher and shriller. Laughter that crackled in your ears. The faraway echo of a tinny, jangling tune.

She saw Margaret pull her father's elbow.

"Say, Dad! How about the roller coaster?"

"Ask your guest. This is her party."

"Hey, Lucy Anne! Wanna go with me 'n' Eileen on the roller coaster?"

"What is it?"

Margaret pointed to a distant gigantic framework against the sky. Its black bars and crossbars looked dangerously fragile. High on top a car full of people—she could see their heads and shoulders—swept around a curve and down out of sight.

"Is there a *track* up there?"

"Sure."

Then the track must be all whirls and curves, ins and outs, ups and downs. Lucy Anne remembered how she had felt on the car that morning.

"No." She shook her head. "I'm not going on that. I'll wait for you."

"We'll all wait for you, outside the entrance." Her father gave Margaret some money. "Then when Lucy Anne has gotten her bearings we'll find something she wants to do."

The two girls darted away. The others followed more slowly, and stopped in a dispirited circle around the ticket booth. Uncle Tom set down the basket of picnic supper he had been carrying.

"Do you see anything you think you would like, Lucy Anne? How about the merry-go-round? You mustn't be bashful, you know, or I'll think you ain't havin' a good time."

"No, Tom. No merry-go-round." Grandmother shook her head. She had not wanted to come on this expedition, and had already grown querulous. "I don't want a sick child on my hands."

"There's a minachoor train—engine and cars— that the little children are crazy about." The sarcastic note was discernible now in Aunt Eleanore's voice. "P'r'aps she'd not be afraid of that."

Lucy Anne flushed indignantly, but it was true. She was afraid.

"It's a right nice little train," her Uncle Tom comforted her. "We'll find it when those wild young-uns come back."

Eileen and Margaret were not gone long. They returned with their hats in their hands, their faces flushed, their hair untidy.

"Oh, it was swell." They were breathless still. "You'd oughta gone."

The party moved on down the boardwalk. Tom Baird bought each of the children a bag of popcorn.

He noticed that Lucy Anne twisted her bag tight shut after she had eaten perhaps a third of it.

"What's the matter, kid? Don't you like it?"

Lucy Anne looked at him and smiled.

"Oh, yes—I love it. I never tasted it before. I thought I would save the rest for Mother."

"Oh, Lord! You eat that, and I'll get some more for Hilary. Here, Margaret—take this nickel and go back to the stand for another sack." He laughed at the thought of his fastidious sister Hilary being offered a greasy five-cent bag of popcorn.

He knew exactly where the little train was, and found the ticket booth for them. Her grandmother bought tickets for Lucy Anne and herself. The other children had scoffed at the idea of wasting time so tamely, and her grandmother would not let Lucy Anne go alone. The two of them went inside the enclosure. The little engine (the engineer towered above it, head, shoulders, chest and arms, as he sat in the driver's cab) had stopped, and scores of very small girls were crowding to get in the cars, shepherded by two women.

"Oh, it's a whole school," said Mrs. Baird, in dismay. "We don't want to get in that crowd. We'll just wait until they have had their ride. Maybe next time there won't be so many."

Lucy Anne had made a motion to join them, but

at her grandmother's words she fell back to her side. She said nothing, but she wished she could have gone with all those others. No one watching, then, could have known that she didn't belong.

The train ran half a dozen times around its flat oval track, and came to a stop at the platform with a puff and a groan and a squeak. All the little girls tumbled out, were formed into lines and led away. No one had joined Lucy Anne and her grandmother, and they alone were waiting. When the platform was clear, Mrs. Baird selected a car in the middle of the train, and they got in.

"Now, you see, we have it all to ourselves. So much better than being crowded." Mrs. Baird fanned herself with the palm-leaf fan which she had carried with her.

No one else came. The engineer looked back at them, incuriously, once. They waited. Still no one came. The engineer looked back again, grinned, released his brakes, pulled the whistle cord, and away they went. Around and around the track, Lucy Anne and her grandmother all alone sitting stiff and upright in the middle of the train. Lucy Anne in those few moments suffered humiliation and chagrin. She felt a thousand eyes watching them go round and round, foolishly, all alone. But not for all the world would she have those eyes see what she felt, because her grandmother had done things the way she thought would please her most. Lucy Anne held her head high, and squeezed her grandmother's hand, as if moved by pleasure and gratitude.

The train stopped. They stood alone on the platform. Once more old Mrs. Baird straightened her hat. They went through the gate marked Exit, and joined the others.

The afternoon dragged wearily on. The straggling little group wandered about aimlessly, as if they were all bored. There was so much noise that it drowned all possible pleasure, and the heat was a tinny, metallic reality, dusty on the tongue. Lucy Anne remembered the sun on the cornfields, the uprush of silence when the car had stopped. That had been in a different world. She was ready for this nightmare to end. She began to limp ostentatiously. Her grandmother soon noticed it, and made them all sit down to rest on some benches beside a little artificial lake, where they fed the swans. Uncle Tom pointed to a group of weeping-willow trees near at hand, and suggested that it was a good spot to picnic, and that they had better get their supper spread before anyone else noticed the trees.

They ate: more bologna, more dank potato salad.

Margaret and Eileen were sent for ice-cream cones. When those were gone, they all sat for a moment in silence, hunched over the tablecloth on the grass, staring listlessly at the debris. Lucy Anne watched her Uncle Tom, who alone looked comfortable: he lay back on the grass, his arms crossed under his head, and watched the yellowing leaves of the willow trees as they moved in the breeze.

The sun went under a cloud. A moment before it had been summer, but now it was autumn. Uncle Tom turned on his side, and yawned.

"When the leaves begin to fall, they'll fall quickly," he said, "it's been dry weather for so long."

"It's going to rain now, shortly." Lucy Anne's grandmother tilted her nose into the air, and sniffed. "I smell it. . . . We must get started. I promised to be back on the seven o'clock car from the city."

The basket was packed, and they turned toward the gate and the street-car line.

Now that the sun had gone, and the wind blew through the open car, it had turned chilly. Lucy Anne was tired and cold and full of sorrow, because the world was different from what she had expected it to be. Her Aunt Eleanore and Margaret and Eileen got off at Greenvale Street, but Uncle Tom went to the city with them. He and her grandmother sat together, and she, in the seat behind them, caught fragments of their conversation.

". . . not altogether a success," her Uncle Tom said.

". . . better to bring Margaret over to our house, where they could really get acquainted . . ." was part of her grandmother's reply.

". . . needs to see more of other children," and Lucy Anne knew that he was speaking of her. "But," he added, "there's plenty of things she could teach Margaret," and then something about "unfortunate influences."

Lucy Anne did not hear her grandmother's answer, but it made him angry.

"I don't mean that. I mean the city—the neighborhood—" He relapsed into silence. She felt sorry for him, because he looked tired, and because he lived in that house in Greenvale Street. When they reached the center of the city, and he helped her off the street car and across the street and up the steps of the big interurban car, she squeezed his hand, because she liked him, and was sorry for him, and said, "Good-bye, Uncle Tom. I had a very nice time at your house, and I wish you and Margaret would come over and see us some time." Afterwards she was uncomfortable because she had not lied and mentioned her Aunt Eleanore too.

As they left the city, Lucy Anne, no longer afraid of the noises of the car, leaned sleepily against her grandmother's shoulder and fell into a doze. She was still cold, but she was too weary to care. She could feel her grandmother shiver, and heard her sneeze.

" 'T's turned colder, hasn't it?" she murmured drowsily. She felt for her mother's bag of popcorn, and found it safe in her lap; she snuggled closer to her grandmother and made no resistance to the sleep that was bearing her down.

Later, she felt her grandmother shaking her. The car had stopped. She sat up and pressed her face against the windowpane. It was pitch-black night outside, but there were lights behind windowpanes, and in the street. They had stopped, then, not in the empty fields far off from anywhere, but on the corner whence that morning they had departed.

"Wake up, child—we're home."

Lucy Anne slipped from the seat and started down the aisle behind her grandmother. She had never in her life been so tired. Her sleepy brain saw a nightmare vision of walking and walking, on and on, on an aching ankle, through the streets, on and on, to the gates of the old house, up the path beneath the maple trees. It was a waking dream of an attempt to reach a place infinitely distant, when you could not put one foot in front of another. She almost fell from the car step into the arms of the conductor, and then was brought wide awake by the splash of raindrops in her face. A storm had come up since the sun had set. She was stunned. It seemed only a few minutes since they had sought the shade of the weeping-willow trees. Her grandmother took her hand. She was muttering something about Aaron. She had told him to meet them if the weather changed. Lucy Anne looked up, through the rain. She had taken off her new hat, and was holding it to her bosom. Aaron was there, on the curb, beside a horse and buggy, holding the hitching rein.

"There he is." Her grandmother had seen him, too.

"Here I is, Miss, I knew no umbrella wouldn't keep you dry through this shower, so I got the horse from the livery stable." He was a little nervous about it. "Miss Hilary, she thought maybe it would be better."

"All right, Aaron. Lift her in, will you? She's half asleep."

There was only one seat in the ramshackle uncurtained buggy. Her grandmother took Lucy Anne on her lap, and Aaron sat on the other side, the reins held loosely in his rheumatic hands. The rain came in on them. Lucy Anne held the bag of popcorn in the crown of her hat. Her grandmother sneezed again, and sniffled. The horse's feet went clop, clop, clop-clop-clop on the paved streets. Raindrops fell from the top of the buggy on to the dashboard. The horse switched his tail across the reins and Aaron jerked them free again. In the light of the carriage lamp, Lucy Anne could see the broad rump rising and falling; it was glistening-sleek in the rain. Clop, Clop. . . .

They stopped, and Aaron got down to unlock the gate. On the driveway the horse's hooves made a different sound, less definite. The clop-clop was blurred at the edges, mushier. That would be because of the mud and weeds, Lucy Anne thought. Aaron drove them through the *porte-cochère* and around to the kitchen door. He helped them down, and then drove away again. The buggy wheels squeaked on the axle as he turned around.

They went into the kitchen. Lucy Anne felt that she had been away for a long while. She had kissed her Aunt Eleanore that morning when she had not wanted to, and now she dared not kiss her mother when she did want to.

Hilary stood beside the stove, where the teakettle was boiling.

"I heard you coming, and came out to make you a cup of tea. You've had your supper, I suppose?"

"Yes, but I should like a cup of hot tea."

"I'll make it. You go on into the library—I built a fire in the grate, so that you could dry yourselves out."

Lucy Anne followed her into the dusky lamplit room. She put her hat on the table, but held the bag of popcorn while she waited. Hilary brought the cup of tea and gave it to her mother.

"Thanks, Hilary. I think I've caught a cold: it was damp on the ground where we ate our supper, and the cars are always drafty." The old woman took her hat off, and sat down with the cup on her knee.

Lucy Anne went to her mother with both hands hidden behind her back.

"I brought you something, Mother."

"Brought me something?" Hilary's thin face softened a little. "Bless you, my child! What is it?"

Lucy Anne gave her the crumpled bag.

"Popcorn!" She laid her hand for a moment on the child's shoulder. "I haven't had a taste of popcorn in years!"

She went to the dining room for a glass bowl, and

poured out the snowy white grains. But she could eat only a little of it, after all. It made her cough.

"I'll have to put it away, I'm afraid, until my cold is better."

Old Mrs. Baird's teacup clattered in the saucer as she put it on the mantelpiece.

"That popcorn will be good and stale before you get over that cold, I think."

The two women looked at each other for a moment. Lucy Anne felt the chill touch of apprehension. She could have wept for weariness. She wanted to go to bed. And her mother could not eat the popcorn. . . .

Hilary's voice was harder when she spoke. It made Lucy Anne jump.

"Did you have a good time?"

Lucy Anne lied valiantly.

"Yes, Mother. I had a very nice time."

"Did you? What did you do all day?"

"In the morning I played with Margaret and a girl named Eileen. In the afternoon we went to an Amusement Park. That's where I got the popcorn—Uncle Tom sent it to you. And Grandmother and I rode on a little train."

"Did you? And how did you like your Uncle Tom and Aunt Eleanore and Cousin Margaret?"

Lucy Anne sighed a little. "Oh, I liked them very much."

Hilary smiled scornfully. Her next question cracked like a whip in the shadowy silent room.

"And how would you like to go and live with them? For always? Be their little girl?"

"Oh, Mother!" She just breathed the reproach. She turned a dead white; her eyes in their black circles of weariness flamed with horror. She turned from her mother to her grandmother. "Gran!" A child's dreadful fear sounded in the little wailing cry.

Mrs. Baird had turned from the fireplace, and was looking at her daughter. Her gray hair straggled about her face; her features looked numb and lifeless, unmolded by the shock, and disintegrated. Hilary had not noticed until that moment how old her mother had grown to look. Her shoulders were bent, her gray head sunk between them. But she stifled quickly the keen pang of pity.

"Hilary!" the old woman muttered. "What an idea to put into the child's head!"

"Your idea, not mine."

Old Mrs. Baird somehow got hold of herself. She mumbled something under her breath, and then turned to Lucy Anne.

"You see, I'm getting old. I can't last forever. Where are you going then?"

"With Mother."

"But suppose she—"

"We'll not suppose anything of the sort," Hilary said coldly.

Her mother said, "I see now why you thought Lucy Anne should make the acquaintance of her cousin. Don't you think"—the old lady breathed hard, sniffling again—"you are a little unscrupulous in your methods?"

Hilary shrugged her shoulders.

"Lucy Anne doesn't know what is good for her. Tom Baird would be a father worth having." Mrs. Baird spoke defiantly.

Lucy Anne broke through the horror which had held her white and silent.

"That house! Oh, no, no, no! Yellow furniture, all knobby! And it *smelled!*"

"But they wouldn't live that way if they had more money. As they will have when I am gone."

Tears streamed down Lucy Anne's cheeks.

"Well, then, don't take on like that. You won't have to go to them if you feel that way about it."

"Oh, Gran!" Lucy Anne whispered her gratitude, then caught her breath, and gulped. "I think I am going to be sick at my stomach. Because they called me a *dago!*" She ran out of the room, and they could hear her open the kitchen door.

"I never could see why Tom married that woman, the lazy slut!" old Mrs. Baird said, finally, with an effort at composure. "The house did smell. It's just as well, perhaps. . . . I'll go and see John Robinson tomorrow. No. Tomorrow's Sunday. Monday, then. But I won't forget the hand you had in this, Hilary Baird."

"We both have something to remember, then. But why should you be so angry with me?"

"Because—because—" she fumbled. She looked very old and tired as she sat there, in the flickering light of the fire. "Because you know so well that I'm not going to do anything to make that child unhappy. And you—you"—she added almost fearfully—"you don't care a straw whether she's happy or not."

Hilary laughed. "You will realize too late that there is only one way to make her happy. . . . Just now I'm going to bring her in out of the rain and take her to bed. She's had a hard day," she added maliciously. "Good night, Mother."

"Good night." The old lady turned and huddled shaking over the fire, but later when she heard Hilary, as she climbed the stairs, coughing, she straightened. "You've got something to think of, young woman. . . . I may outlast you yet."

The Sunday that followed was a gloomy day, damp and raw. The wind blew fitfully, and sudden gusts of rain beat against the windows. In the maple trees about the house, bluejays squalled and scolded. A flock of blackbirds on the way south found shelter in the treetops, and the cracked chorus of their voices was borne to the house on the wind. Mrs. Baird hated them, and the noise made her restless, but she could not ask Aaron to shoot them on Sunday. All morning she moved from one window to another, complaining.

Mrs. Baird always spent Sunday afternoon in the stiff rocking chair in the library, dressed in her black silk dress without an apron, with her Bible open in her lap. On this Sunday she put on the black dress and brought out the Bible, but her cold was so much worse that her eyes watered and streamed with tears. She was forced to ask Lucy Anne to read to her.

On Monday she was no better, but she rose betimes and washed the clothes and hung them in the laundry to dry, and by dinner time was carefully dressed in her street clothes. It was raining again, a steady downpour. Hilary tried to dissuade her from going out, but she was adamant.

"This is the sort of thing that it is better not to postpone, once you've made up your mind. You never know what may happen."

"Then at least have Aaron get the horse from the livery stable again. You will be soaked through, if you don't—"

"Nonsense. I'm not so old yet that I'm afraid of a little rain."

Hilary and Lucy Anne were alone in the house all afternoon, Hilary on the couch, Lucy Anne at work on the arithmetic problems that her grandmother had set her to do. The two were not altogether at ease with each other. Lucy Anne wanted to ask her mother what her grandmother had meant about her cough, but she did not dare. She was not sure whether she was afraid of being rebuffed by her mother, or afraid of being told. She worked at her problems in silence until they were finished and neatly copied, and then she went to the window to watch for her grandmother, and to watch Aaron shoot the blackbirds.

He stood under the trees, careless of the rain, his rifle under his arm. Now and again he pointed it into the treetops and fired. Lucy Anne watched and listened: after the crack of the rifle came the sudden rushing windy noise of the birds' wings, beating free of the leaves, rising above the branches, and the sound of their voices crying, clamorous above the house. . . . But they always came back to the trees, after a while, and Aaron would point his rifle into the treetops again.

It was late in the afternoon when she saw her grandmother coming up the brick path. She asked her mother if she should make her a cup of tea. "It's pouring down," she explained.

"Yes, put the kettle on to boil." Hilary smiled.

Mrs. Baird came in, out of breath and gasping.

"I walked so fast I've a pain in my side," she said, as she dropped into the chair by the fire. "Touch of pleurisy, I shouldn't wonder." She took off her wet shoes and placed them on the fender. Her stockings had white heels and white toes: the white now was water-stained and yellow. Lucy Anne brought the cup of tea, carrying it with both hands, and offered it to her gravely.

"Thank you, my darling. How good and hot!" She wiped her eyes and blew her nose.

"If you still have that 'touch of pleurisy' in the morning, you had better send Aaron for Dr. Martin, Mother."

"If I'm not better in the morning, I shouldn't be surprised if I would." Mrs. Baird made the grudging admission with a glance at Hilary, on the distant couch, and Hilary knew at once that her mother was really ill.

"Did you see Mr. Robinson?" she asked.

"Yes, I saw him. Obstinate old fool. Argued with me all afternoon. He was glad enough to change my will, but he didn't like the changes I suggested. I made 'em, all the same." She chuckled hoarsely, and added, "You always were a great favorite of his, Hilary."

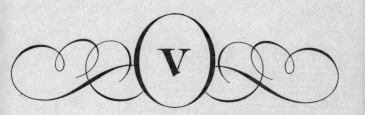

1

O N THE NEXT MORNING, MRS. BAIRD WAS
SO MUCH WORSE THAT SHE MADE NO AT-
TEMPT TO GET OUT OF HER BED. SHE
breathed hoarsely and with difficulty, and coughed,
a loose rattling cough. Hilary sent for Dr. Martin,
who came, and listened to her explanation with
scarcely a word for her or Lucy Anne.

"The town is full of influenza," he said, "she's
picked it up somewhere. I have scores of cases,
myself, and spend my time running from one patient to another in order to squeeze them all into
one day."

Hilary led him into the bedroom, and then waited, in the hall. When he came out, he looked so serious that Lucy Anne was frightened, and went into the library and closed the door behind her.

"Well?" said Hilary. "She thinks herself that it is pleurisy."

"Pleurisy!" Dr. Martin repeated, scornfully. "It's bronchitis, if it must have a name. . . . No, Hilary, it's worse than that. I'm afraid it is going to be bronchial pneumonia."

"Pneumonia! But pneumonia at her age—"

"Exactly. Pneumonia at her age is a very serious business. She is not very ill—I mean dangerously ill—now—but she must have the best of care." He looked at Hilary gravely, and saw that she appreciated the irony of his statement. She had let him know, once, that her mother's death was her way to freedom. She flushed a little under his scrutiny.

"You would be afraid, wouldn't you, to leave her in my hands?"

"No. I was only thinking—"

"You would have kept on thinking, too, I know. No, you must find a nurse for her, and then, whatever happens—"

"That would be best, for you at any rate. You aren't equal to the strain of nursing her yourself. I'll have a nurse here sometime this morning, and I shall return myself late this afternoon." He told Hilary what she was to do with the medicines that he was leaving.

"And—do you think I should send for my brothers?"

"No-o. No, she isn't so ill as all that. But if I were you I should write to them and let them know about the pneumonia—just to be on the safe side. You never know what old people's hearts are going to do."

Hilary went in to tell her mother that a nurse was coming; she had expected her to be difficult, but old Mrs. Baird was that morning too concentrated on the necessity of getting her breath to care what went on in the house, or who was there. When the nurse arrived, she was accepted with the same indifference. She was a gentle, quiet, elderly woman, with an air of sure competence within the sickroom, and one of deprecating bewilderment when its doors had closed behind her.

Hilary left her with Mrs. Baird, and went into the library to write the letters to her brothers. Lucy Anne was there, trying to read. She rose when her mother entered, and went to meet her.

"How is she?"

"Oh—no worse, at any rate. Don't be frightened,

Lucy Anne. There is a nurse to look after her now, and Dr. Martin.''

"I know—but—but—will she be sick for a long while?''

"Yes, weeks and weeks. It takes a long while to have pneumonia and get over it.''

"Then shall I have a holiday from my lessons?''

Hilary laughed. "I'm afraid you will. I shall not have time for them with all the other things I must do.''

In a day's time they had settled down to the new routine, and in a little while it was as if they had never known anything different. The nurse had slept on a cot in Mrs. Baird's bedroom, and she had her meals with Lucy Anne and Hilary, because her patient was not so ill that she could not be left alone. Hilary cooked and washed dishes and kept the house clean, and Lucy Anne wiped the dishes and dusted, and when those tasks were done, she was left to her own devices. Hilary was too busy for part of the day, and thereafter too exhausted to pay much attention to the child. She was always on hand, morning and evening, to see Dr. Martin when he came, and he was never too hurried or tired to talk with her for a minute, but when he had gone she crept away somewhere, and did not appear again until mealtime.

Hilary heard from her brothers. Will could not leave New York unless it were absolutely imperative. She was so disappointed when she read his letter that she realized how much she had longed to see him. Once he had been almost like a second father to her, but, like all the others, he had not forgiven her her marriage, and she had not seen him now for five years. Not since she had left New York . . . five years ago, when love and pride had fought within her, and love had lost.

But Tom would come to see his mother on Saturday afternoon, when he was free. Hilary smiled rather bitterly at the thought of Tom, who had been forgiven his *mésalliance* because Eleanore had been possessed of the one virtue that Paolo had lacked. But there are worse things to be faced in matrimony, Hilary thought, than occasional unfaithfulness. When she saw Tom, she knew that she was right. On the surface he was affable, and casual in his manner toward her, but he could not conceal that look he bore of one defeated. She saw that even Lucy Anne felt sorry for him, and she tried to shield him from the child's pitying gaze. After all, she and Tom had grown up in the old house together, and when they stood side by side at the foot of their mother's bed, it was easy to remember what the three of them had been to each other once, two young children and their middle-aged mother. Now Tom was tired and shabby, and she was tired and ill, and their mother was an old woman propped on a pillow, with straggling wisps of hair, breathing heavily. "And," thought Hilary, "I am the only one of them all who has found anything in life worth finding: it is less futile to love a dead man than to have ceased to love a living woman." And she supposed that Tom despised and pitied her.

2

NOW WHEN NO ONE NOTICED WHAT SHE
DID OR WHERE SHE WENT, LUCY ANNE
SPENT ALL HER DAYS IN THE FRONT
drawing room. Early in the morning, when the
breakfast dishes had been wiped and put away, she
was allowed to see her grandmother, for a moment,
and after that no one thought of her until mealtime.

Her fear and her dread and her pity and her
repugnance all strove to master her in those few
seconds every day that she spent at her grandmother's bedside; she choked them all down, and
stood outwardly calm and controlled, but with a

white face and eyes wide and black, and a strained look about the mouth. She was always able to smile, and to hold her grandmother's hand, and answer "Yes, Gran," or "No, Gran," to her questions. She could not always understand what her grandmother said, because her teeth were not in her mouth, but in a glass of water on the table beside the bed. Lucy Anne always tried not to look at the glass full of teeth. She had never in her life before seen her grandmother without them, nor had she ever seen her before undressed, with the frill of her night-gown loose about her wrinkled sunken neck, or with her hair down in two thin, untidy gray plaits. She every morning restrained with difficulty her sigh of relief when the nurse told her she must go.

Every morning she went into the drawing room and opened the shutters over one window, and curled up on the chair that stood where the light came in. There was no use even thinking of going out of doors. It had hardly stopped raining once since her grandmother had first caught her cold. "The worst October since 1880," Dr. Martin had said, and had laughed; she supposed it was a joke, but the rain did not seem funny to her. October was usually the most beautiful month of the year, but—though she longed to see the sun with a passionate longing—she thought that it was fitting that it should rain now, because her grandmother was going to die.

From the first morning when Dr. Martin had to come to see her, Lucy Anne had been sure that her grandmother was going to die. Had she not said herself, "I'm getting old," and "I can't last forever"? And who should know, if not Grandmother herself?

Now Lucy Anne was waiting. She supposed that her grandmother was waiting too. Oddly enough, it was her mother who did not seem to expect anything to happen, who went on doing the ordinary things as ordinarily as possible.

Crouched in the big chair in the drawing room, day after day, Lucy Anne waited. Sometimes, because she was so frightened of death, she clenched her hands and closed her eyes and thought with all the strength of her being, "No—no—no! Please, dear Grandmother—please get well, so that everything can be the same as it was before." She would think of things as they had been before, and the tears would fall on her cheeks, and she would find herself crying.

Sometimes she thought of Lissa and Nellie and Mary Jane, and of playing games with them. But she could not imagine games, now—she could only see them sitting, like herself, in the other chairs in the

drawing room—chairs in the shadowed corners—
chairs so much too large for them, that their feet did
not touch the floor, but stuck straight out in front
of them. They looked at Lucy Anne and she looked
at them, and they whispered together. And Lucy
Anne whispered, "Good-bye, Lissa. Good-bye, all
of you," because she knew now that when her
grandmother died they would all be gone. All the
voices and the echoes of laughter would be gone
out of the old house. She had thought that it was she
who had made them come alive, but it had been her
grandmother, after all, and no one else could, because no one else remembered them. And so she
whispered, "Good-bye, Lissa," and wept because
they would so soon be forgotten, like all the others
who had been forgotten. But never once through
all those days did Lucy Anne think of the graveyard,
and all the graves there that had been forgotten: not
because the memory was not there, on the threshold
of her mind, ready to enter, but because she so
resolutely closed the door on it, and held it fast.

Sometimes she spent the day thinking of what
would happen to her afterwards. She was to be with
her mother: her grandmother had promised her
that. And her mother knew that she was going to be
a musician. Lucy Anne always held her breath and
leaped past that place in her thoughts; she knew that

she was wicked, because when she thought of being a musician nothing else seemed to matter much—not even her grandmother—and so she jumped the thought, and what followed she called "pretending," because that made it seem less wicked than if it had been "hoping." On one day she would pretend that she and her mother lived there alone in the house, and she had music lessons from Miss Collins, and played on the rosewood piano; she would pretend that they had opened the house, and had it full of people—nice people, like Dr. Martin, with parties and picnics under the trees in the summer. On the next day she would pretend—and she found it much more exciting—that her mother had taken her back to the house where she was born, and that there in the garden with the fig tree and the fountain on the wall, she was learning to sing.

And then she would remember, suddenly, in the middle of her pretending, that her grandmother was dying, and she would clench her hands and put her head down on her knees and whisper, "Oh, no, no—"

Until one morning when Dr. Martin came out of her grandmother's room into the library, where she and her mother were waiting, and he was beaming and triumphant, and said, "She is much better today, you know. I think she will do now."

"Thanks to you," Hilary said. "Sit down with us and rest, if you have won your battle."

"But I have other patients who aren't doing so well." And the worried, drawn look came back to his face. "I'm sorry—I'd like to stop for a minute. . . . What's the matter, Lucy Anne? Aren't you glad to hear that your grandmother is going to get well?" He could see that she was shaking as if with a chill, and he laid his hand on her shoulder.

"Are you *sure?*" The question was hardly more than a whisper.

"Oh, we are never sure, we doctors, no matter how much we pretend. But if nothing unexpected happens she will get well. That is almost being sure, isn't it?" He turned again to Hilary. "Her heart is still in an uncertain state, and a bad shock might kill her. But there is no reason to suppose—I mean, she is having the best of care—"

"Yes—but did you tell her how much better she is? You did? Then the best of care may not continue. I mean, she will dismiss the nurse, and you nor all the king's horses and all the king's men could stop her."

When Dr. Martin had gone, the nurse came out of Mrs. Baird's bedroom in search of Hilary. She looked bewildered and hurt.

"Dr. Martin told Mrs. Baird that she was better

and would soon be well, and now"—she said—"now she thinks she doesn't need me any longer."

"I knew it." Hilary sighed. "It was surprising that she would consent to have a nurse at all."

"I wish you would talk with her."

Hilary went in to argue with her mother, but the old lady considered herself once more the head of the household.

"I don't like strangers about me, and you know it. It's a pity you can't take care of me now."

"I can do my best, but as a nurse I am not very satisfactory."

"I don't need much nursing now. No—she's been here long enough."

"But Mother—she's been engaged for at least two more weeks."

"Pay her for them, and let her have a holiday. If she is still here this afternoon—"

"Oh, not this afternoon—wait until the doctor comes back, and I can ask him—"

"Ask him nothing!" old Mrs. Baird croaked angrily. "I'll not have that woman here any longer, prying."

"Oh, Mother, she's so inoffensive—" But Hilary broke off at the sight of her mother's distorted white face. "Oh, very well. But if you get worse again, we shall have to have her back."

"I'm not going to get worse. I shall be up in a few days. . . . How much is there to pay? Bring me my checkbook and a pen."

Mrs. Baird signed the check which Hilary wrote for her, and the nurse packed her clothes and departed. Hilary awaited Dr. Martin with some trepidation; he was amazed and horrified when, that evening, she told him the nurse had gone.

"But she might have a bad heart attack—"

"She would have had one, on the spot, if I had opposed her."

"But, Hilary! It is too much for you. I can't allow it."

Hilary merely shrugged her shoulders. He went into the sickroom to take Mrs. Baird to task.

"I couldn't stand her any longer," the old lady explained, "meechin' in and out like a white rat. And," she added, with a keen look up at the doctor, "you needn't worry about me—Hilary isn't going to poison my soup."

"It's Hilary I'm worrying about," he replied stiffly. "She isn't equal to it."

"Oh, nonsense. She's none so delicate as you think. And it's a shame if she can't do this one thing for me, after all these years."

He gave up then, and left her, and left the house.

An impossible old woman, he thought, and his heart ached for Hilary; he wondered how long this unholy seesaw between the two women could go on. The time had almost come when he might again venture to ask Hilary to marry him.

3

WHEN A FEW DAYS LATER HE CAME FOR
HIS MORNING CALL AT THE HOUSE,
NO ONE ANSWERED HIS KNOCK AT
the door. He opened it, finally, and walked in, and
crossed the hall to the library, and there found Hilary lying in her leather chair. She looked up at him
as he entered, but did not move. She lay like a stone,
her face white and her cheeks sunken. His heart
stopped at the sight of her, but he said, with his
ordinary composure, "Didn't you hear me knock?"

She nodded. "But I couldn't have got up—not
just then."

"Where is the brandy I brought for your mother?"

"On the sideboard in the dining room."

He brought her a glass of brandy, and waited, after she had drunk it, until the blood washed back into her face.

"Hilary," he asked her then, gently, "what end do you see to all this?"

She smiled faintly.

"Let's not put it into words."

"That's what I am going to do. In the first place, your mother will be well in a few more weeks—"

"You say so." She shivered. "But I have a strange, queer feeling about it—as if she wouldn't."

"She will, I tell you, barring accidents." He spoke almost angrily. As a professional man he disliked having his verdict doubted. "But by the time she is out of bed, you will be in yours. Do you see any escape for yourself?"

"No. But you know, it is rather peaceful to say to one's self 'hopeless' and to be willing to let it go at that."

"There is an alternative, if you can face it."

"You aren't going to ask me again to marry you?"

"Yes, I am." He drew himself up, and from his

great height looked down at her, so slight and pale and pitiful. "Wouldn't even that be better?"

"I told you before"—she gestured wearily—"I do not love you."

"Of course not. You couldn't, ill as you are, not anyone. But if you were well, you don't know that you couldn't, then."

She was silent, and he pressed his advantage.

"Think, Hilary. We could go to New Mexico. That is one thing about being a doctor, you know"—he spoke cheerfully now, easily—"he can practice as well in one place as another. After a while you would be as well as anyone—"

"Is that a promise?" Her eyelids flickered in the quick glance she gave him; he felt that he was being mocked.

"No. Not a promise . . . but a sure hope." He frowned a little, but his eyes were tender. "Won't you let me do what I can for you?"

"And Lucy Anne?"

"She would go with us, of course."

"She would be happy—"

"I think she would. You would have nothing to reproach yourself with on that score. I can promise you that."

"I am not so sure. But—"

"You will? Oh, Hilary!" His heart lifted. Gently

and lightly he ran his fingers the length of her arm. This was not the Hilary of whom he had dreamed so long, this white and broken woman, but he loved her dearly.

"I—think—that I will. But"—she added hastily—"I must have today to think it over. Tomorrow morning I will tell you, once and for all."

He stooped then, and picked her up, easily as if she had been a child, and carried her to the couch.

"Stay here all day today, while you are thinking it over . . . I mean it—those are doctor's orders. I was afraid you were on the verge of collapse when I came in . . . No, now listen: not a word. I will send my cook here to get lunch for you—give her the padlock key and everything, and your mother need never know that she's in the house. I can get my lunch uptown. And Lucy Anne must do everything for her grandmother that she can possibly do. Where is Lucy Anne?"

"In the front drawing room, I expect. Thinking of graveyards." Hilary laughed. "Open the door in the hall and call her."

But Lucy Anne came in before he had gone: she knew that it was time for him to be there. He told her that her mother was tired, and was not to be disturbed to wait on Mrs. Baird unless it was absolutely necessary, and he left her like an unfledged Saint Michael on guard at the library door.

To Hilary from that moment the day seemed enveloped in a kind of fog—a fog of sleep and fever. She was vaguely conscious that out of doors it was raining and that the wind was blowing. The old colored woman who cooked for Dr. Martin came in through the kitchen door. Hilary heard her whispering to Lucy Anne in the hall, and thus learned that the child was still there, sitting cross-legged, she supposed, on the threshold of the closed door. Later, she heard Aaron and the woman gossiping in the kitchen, and wondered if her mother could hear, too. She was in her mother's room, once or twice, that morning, but nothing was said.

Once, late in the morning, she rose and went out to the laundry. Almost without knowing how she had got there, she found herself standing, half-dazed, beside the laundry stove, one of the stove lids lifted on the hook she held in her hand. Early in the day she had built a fire there, in order to heat the irons for the big pile of clothes that she had washed the day before, and the fire had not yet burnt itself out. She heard the wind in the chimney, and she wondered if one could build so huge a fire in that stove that the sparks would fly out the chimney, and whether those sparks would set fire to the laundry roof, and whether the arrival of the fire department would be a shock to anyone with a bad heart. It was not an idea in her mind, it was a nightmare; she wakened from it, replaced the stove lid, and returned to the couch in the library.

Lucy Anne brought her her lunch on a tray, and afterwards she slept. Half asleep and half awake, she thought of her husband, and flung a challenge at him: *"What can you do about it?"* Then, as if the unspoken words were echoing in the air about her, she started up with the remorseful cry "Paolo!" on her lips, and thought how odd it was that she could so miss from the house one who had never been there. It was that appalling emptiness of the house that revealed to her her own mind: with Paolo gone from it, her mind would be as empty as the house. She rose and drew up a chair to the table and sat down to write a note to Dr. Martin. She had not once that day given her thought to him, but without thinking she knew now that it would be impossible for her to marry him.

4

It was long that night before Hilary slept. She lay on her back, her hands crossed nunlike over her breasts, and listened to the tumult of the wind as it swooped from the clouded night sky and howled about the chimneys of the old house. She could hear each blast as, from a long way off, it seemed to draw itself together for the attack, as the roar of its coming gathered momentum and sounded deafeningly its threat, as it dropped for an instant, and then fell upon windows and walls with a terrible concussion. The walls did not tremble; the old brick house was too sturdily built; but the doors and windows rattled, an unbearable recurrent staccato, punctuated sometimes by the crash of a shutter blown back against the wall. After each gust there was a pause, a breathless moment of waiting, when she could hear again the silence of the dark rooms and the stairways that were walled away from the wind, the faint cracking of old wood settling into place, the squeak of a stair tread. The door from her room to the porch was closed, but in those silences, she could hear on the porch floor the slow scrape-scrape of a dried leaf that had blown from the grapevine on the pillars. Then another blast of wind would rise and gather its strength and fall upon the house, and the sound of a moving leaf would be lost in the tumult. The leaf itself would be lifted up and whirled in an eddy out and away between the pillars, tossed to a distant oblivion on the night wind.

Hilary lay and thought about the wind and the dried leaf scraping on the porch floor, because they were in essence changeless, and in them her thoughts could have rest. Ordinarily on such a night she would have pulled the end of the pillow she was not sleeping on close to her face, and would have rested her cheek on it, as if it had been her husband's shoulder, but tonight she lay staring at the ceiling.

She had lost her husband, for had she not that day betrayed him? For hours she had known that she could not marry Martin Child, and she had that evening sent Aaron with the note that told him so, but she had not expected that the recantation would bring her back Paolo. Betrayal is betrayal, be it ever so brief.

But because she refused to think of these things, but let go her hold on all reality save the sound of the night wind rushing about the earth as it turned slowly toward the morning, she did finally fall into a profound slumber. Blast after blast of wind bent the treetops and sent dead boughs crashing to the earth, assaulted the house and rattled the windows, tore all the leaves save two or three from the grapevine and sent them eddying on the unquiet air, but Hilary slept.

She slept until the wild horror-stricken cry of a child rang through the house. Then she was out of bed and in her dressing gown all in an instant, and lighted her bedside lamp with a trembling hand.

It was Lucy Anne who had cried out, but where was she? Not in her own room: the cry had come from somewhere farther away. With her lamp held high in one hand, the dressing gown gathered up from her feet in the other, she stepped into the hall. The door into the front part of the house was ajar.

She slipped through it and along the dark corridor to the great paneled staircase. The lamp, dim as it seemed in the vast depth of shadow, lighted the marks of small bare feet in the dust of the stairs. Hilary leaned over the banisters. Lucy Anne was crouched on the bottom step, her hands on the newel post, as if she were hiding behind it. Hilary put the lamp on the floor, and ran down to her.

"What was it, my child? What kind of nightmare did you have that sent you walking in your sleep?"

Lucy Anne turned to her mother, her face gray with terror, her eyes profound and black as the shadows that circled about and behind her.

"Mother," she whispered, "he frightened me."

"Who? . . . Come back to bed, you ridiculous baby. . . . Come with me and hop into my bed, and tell me what you dreamed."

Slowly Lucy Anne pulled herself to her feet.

"It wasn't a dream."

"Come, child. I can't carry you."

"Walk close to me. I am afraid." She drew her breath sharply between her teeth.

Hilary laid her hand on her shoulder. She could feel her trembling, and her flesh was cold to the touch. An icy quivering crept down her own spine. In the silence of the deserted rooms, in the shadows that rose and fell with the flickering of the lamp on the floor above them there was something eerie and queer, something not quite to be explained away by the tale of a childish nightmare. She resisted the compulsion to look over her shoulder as they climbed the stairs.

Hilary picked up the lamp and led Lucy Anne back to her room; she put the lamp on the table and tucked the child into her bed, and herself sat at her feet and drew the corner of her eiderdown over her knees.

"Now, Lucy Anne, tell me about it. Why did you get out of bed, if you weren't dreaming?"

"It was the music playing." Visibly she fought for self-control. "Didn't you hear it?"

"No." Hilary smiled a little. "There wasn't any to hear. Of course you dreamed it."

"You were asleep then, or you would have heard. You see, I wasn't asleep. I was awake listening. Listening to the wind getting ready to come back again and try to shake the house, and listening to a dead leaf scraping on the brick path. Scrape, it would go, and then stop, and then scrape, scrape again. And then I heard the music." Lucy Anne spoke slowly, weighing her words, living over again those moments when she had got out of her bed, striving to compel her mother to give her story credence.

"At first I thought it must be outside," she continued, "so I went to the window and listened, but there was nothing there but the wind. Then I knew it was the piano."

"The piano! Downstairs?"

"Yes. So I went through the hall to the stairs, and down the stairs without making any noise. And I came nearer and nearer to the music. It was like something calling in the wind—calling and waiting, and calling and waiting. But I knew it was not calling for me, so I tiptoed to the door to watch."

"And did you see?"

"Yes. It was a man there playing. I couldn't see anything but his back, and sometimes his hand, and his hair. Black shining hair."

"But how could you see?" Hilary's voice was flat in its effort at restraint. "It was dark downstairs. Pitch-black night. Or did you dream a lamp, too?"

"There was no lamp," Lucy Anne shook her head, puzzled. "But there was light enough to see him and Grandmother when she came in."

"Grandmother?"

"Yes. He was calling her. I knew it as soon as I saw her. She oughtn't to have come, ought she? Because she looked so sick. Her hair was down, and she—she hadn't—put her teeth in. So that she couldn't speak clearly, but only mumbled."

"Your nightmare had all the elements of the grotesque." Hilary put her hand on Lucy Anne's knee, and tried to laugh. It would have been better if she had not tried. She said quickly, "What did Grandmother say when she mumbled?"

"She said, 'What do you want with me?' And he didn't say anything, only laughed, and began playing something else. Something terrible because it was so happy and so—so—*triumphant.* It was terrible like battles—like 'with the hoofs of his horses shall he tread down all thy streets—' " Her voice trailed off into a whisper. Her wide eyes, distended with horror, stared far off beyond her mother. Then with a quick gesture, she pushed the heavy black hair back from her face. "Mother," she insisted, "how could I have dreamed music like that? I can still hear it. It went like this—" She whistled a few bars softly.

Hilary stiffened, rose to her feet, stood as if turned to stone.

"The 'Turkish March.' " She too spoke in a whisper, now. "How—how blatant. But it's just what he would have played. . . . But you could have dreamed it," she added quickly. "You heard him play it often enough long ago when you were little."

"Heard who play it?"

"Your father. Surely you knew you were dreaming about your own father?"

"Yes, I knew who it was."

"He played it the night I promised him—"

"Promised him what?"

"That whatever happened, you would be a musician some day." The two looked at each other. Lucy Anne was frightened, now, for her mother. The lines beside her mouth had gone so deep they lay in shadow. Her face might have been chiseled out of stone, it was so immobile, its angles were so hard. "But, don't you see, Lucy Anne, if it had been really he, and not a dream, he would have played for me? . . . To remind me. . . ." Hilary spoke urgently, as if to reassure herself. Lucy Anne was sorry for her but she shook her head.

"You had given me to Grandmother. Hadn't you?" she demanded inexorably.

"Only for while she lived. Afterwards—" She stopped short, and seated herself again on the foot of the bed. "Why did you cry out?"

"That was a long while afterwards. . . . While he played, I stood waiting in the door. When he finished, Grandmother said again, 'What do you want of me?' And he stood up and motioned her to a chair, and took up a violin and a bow from on top of the piano. And he said, 'I have come to play for you once more before you die.' And he put the violin under his chin and played on it." Lucy Anne was sobbing now, quietly. Hilary, who had held her breath for a moment, let it go in a long sigh. Once more she put her hand on the child's shoulder, and waited for Lucy Anne to be able to continue.

"And what was that like, the music on the violin?" she asked finally.

"I—I don't think I can tell you, Mother. . . . It was as if the most beautiful thing in the world were lost. And the music was hunting for it and wanting it and singing for it, but never finding it, but it was there in the music, too, the most beautiful thing, but always running away."

Slowly Hilary's hand slipped down from Lucy Anne's shoulder. Her lips trembled. She rose to her feet again, still and hushed, as if listening.

"Paolo!" The whisper hung echoing in the lamp-lit room. She turned, ran to the porch door, and threw it open. Lucy Anne saw the wind come into the room, sweep back her mother's dressing gown, lift it in billowing waves from the floor, touch her hair, blow it back from her mother's face.

Hilary went out on the porch. Then her low cry of despair, too, was blown back into the room.

"Paolo!" Then for a long while there was silence,

except for the wind, and then again the murmured name: "Paolo!"

Lucy Anne waited, lying frozen in the still hand of terror. Her mother was crying, out there on the porch. From somewhere in the background of her mind sounded the words "and midnight shall be a witness to my tears. . . ."

Finally she heard her mother's step on the threshold. She closed the door, then came and stood over the child.

"Listen, Lucy Anne. It was a dream you dreamed. If it had been really your father, he would have come to me. Surely. . . ." The voice broke, stopped, steadied, went on. "For a moment"—and she dared to laugh—"for a moment I was almost mad enough to believe that you had been seeing ghosts." Hilary eyed the child with fierce scorn, then, with a long breath, she drew herself up as though to dismiss the subject. "But before we have forgotten all this," she said, "there is one thing that I must say, and that is that love is a terrible thing. Whether you are his daughter, and would break other people's lives, or whether you are mine, and would break your own, love is a terrible thing. Avoid it."

With a quick gesture she lifted the lamp from the table and held it close above Lucy Anne, who shrank away from her into the pillows.

"Do you hear?"

"Yes, Mother." The terrified child whimpered a little.

"Promise?"

"Yes, Mother, I promise."

"Very well." Hilary put the lamp down. "Then we need never speak of it again. Now go on and tell me the rest of the dream. He played. . . . When he finished?"

"When he finished, Grandmother said, 'You know very well, Paolo, that anyone who has listened to you play can refuse you nothing. What do you want of me?'

"And he said 'Lucy Anne,' and he smiled—oh, a terrible smile, like the first music he played, and so I screamed, and there wasn't any light, any longer, and I ran. But it was so dark, and I was so frightened, that I couldn't go any farther than the foot of the stairs."

"You screamed and woke up, that was what really happened." But Lucy Anne had reached the end of her endurance.

"Mother, what does it mean?" she cried, and once more began to sob hysterically.

"Don't cry. By daylight it won't mean anything." Hilary lay down beside her, and took her head on her shoulder. But before the last of the child's sobs had been choked back, she was out and on her feet again.

"I never thought—how dreadful—that scream! I wonder if your grandmother heard it and was frightened. I must go down and see. You may stay here in my bed until I come back, if you like."

But Hilary did not come back that night.

She took the lamp, and after pausing for a moment at the head of the back stairs, to fight her reluctance, she went down.

Her mother's bed was empty. A lamp on the stand beside it was burning with a thick dark flame that had smoked the chimney black.

She crossed the hall and opened the door that led to the drawing room. Holding her lamp in both hands, she lifted it until the light streamed across the long dark room.

Her mother was sitting in one of the sheeted wing chairs. Her head was thrown back and her mouth had fallen open. Hilary had no need to go further to know that she was dead.

1

D R. MARTIN WAS NOT SURPRISED AT THE NOTE FROM HILARY THAT AARON LEFT AT THE DOOR. IT BROUGHT TO AN END an impossible dream, and if for a little while, he had believed, it was only as one deludes oneself into believing, once or twice in a lifetime, that the impossible can become possible. When he had read it, he sat down at his solitary hearth and took out his pipe for consolation. He sat nursing the bowl of the pipe in one hand, the other hung over the arm of the chair with Hilary's note between the fingers.

"DEAR DR. MARTIN," she had written, "It was very wrong of me to have allowed you to cherish for even these few hours a false hope. I am sorry—believe me, I am sorry. But it is impossible. It would be too queer—don't you see that it would—*you* and *me?* It frightens me to think how I might have wakened one morning when it was too late, and seen then how nightmarishly queer it was. It is not that I, Hilary, might not have loved you, Martin, each of us being what we are. But my life has gone so far in one direction, and yours has gone so far in another, that they cannot be made to come together now. Anyone's life is incoherent enough, distorted enough, without attempting to bring extraneous elements into it. This is not what I should say, if I would have you understand, but I can't find the words. I was mad for a moment, and now I am sane and sorry: that is really enough to say.

"HILARY."

Dr. Martin smiled a crooked smile on one side of his mouth as he sucked at his pipe. He understood, he thought, only too well. In Hilary's life his love was only an irrelevant episode, and it would soon be blotted out. But that same love had become in his own life the motif that sounded through all.

He knocked the ash from his pipe on the bars of the grate, filled it again, and once more leaned back in his chair.

His life would be no different. That was what seemed strange to him that night. This note which had seemed to change everything, had in reality changed nothing. Tomorrow would be like yesterday; next month, in its comings in and goings out, like last month. His life must be kept to its pattern. Unromantic sanity, that was the pattern. Kindness, imperturbability. The meaningless tenderness of the medical man. He grimaced. Tonight he would sit here before the fire and burn out of his mind his dreams and his love.

Sometime late in the night he laid the note on the fire. He murmured "Hilary" just once as he watched it burn, as though there were a kind of midnight magic in the name. He made no motion to leave his chair; only the dawn of another day—the day that would be like all his other days save the one just past—could end his vigil.

But as the hours slipped away he began to feel that the note had given him something back, not taken it away. His portrait of Hilary: it was restored to him, and not destroyed in the flames. In his sorrow there was mingled an element of rejoicing. Hilary had escaped surrender, still she remained the undefeated. For years of his life he had imagined one Hilary, and in his wooing he had found another; now he had learned at last that, after all, he had from the very beginning seen the truth: he had seen in her an uncompromising certainty and a flamelike clarity of mind and an intensity of purpose which would ever deny defeat. And if he loved her for all the rest of his life, he would love this woman whom he had imagined, his dreams unmarred by any memory of disillusionment.

He had not been surprised when Aaron brought the note, but when his bell pealed again just before daylight, and he found the old negro once more on the doorstep, he was shocked and startled. He brought him into the room where he had been sitting, where the fire still flickered on the hearth, and where the air was blue with tobacco smoke.

Aaron's face was ashen in the light, a dead gray, his eyes blurred with tears. He held his hat before him, tight in the grip of his twisted, knotty fingers.

"Ol' Miss, she's gone!"

"Gone! What do you mean, Aaron?"

"Dead, sir! Dead!"

"How can—! What happened?"

"Don't know, sir. Miss Hilary told me—told me to fetch the doctor, right smart."

"I'll come at once."

He backed his car from the garage, picked Aaron up, turned through the sleeping town toward the Baird place.

Hilary was in the drawing room with her mother's body, and the doctor found her there. He was horrified—by her face, as well as by the unexpectedness of Mrs. Baird's death. What had happened in the old house that night? He dared not look at Hilary; he sent her from the room.

Heart failure. Not perhaps to be wondered at, as he had warned them. But—

He sought Hilary in the library. She was in the chair beside the fire; she was dressed, and there was nothing distraught in her appearance, yet he hesitated on the threshold. She was white as death, and her translucent pallor frightened him. But she looked up and motioned for him to enter.

"What happened, Hilary?"

There was in her somber gray eyes the look of burnt-out fires, fires that had flamed to exhaustion behind the mask of her face. She did not try to smile, nor to greet him.

"It was Lucy Anne." Her dry lips moved stiffly.

"I am afraid—afraid of what she will feel if she knows."

He drew up beside her the small desk chair, and stood for a minute with his hands on its back. His voice when he spoke was gentle and reassuring.

"You haven't told me what happened."

Hilary stirred slightly in her chair, smiled a little.

"You have been frightened, haven't you? Thinking perhaps that it was I—but it wasn't. Lucy Anne had a dream and walked in her sleep. It was the wind, perhaps—that storm. In the middle of the night I heard her scream, and I got up and found her at the foot of the stairs—the front stairs, where we never go. I took her upstairs and put her in my bed, and she told me what she had dreamed." He saw her hands tighten on the arms of the chair until the knuckles went white. Her eyes clung to his for an instant. He sat down and put his hand on hers. "It was pretty bad for a child," she continued. "I didn't wonder that she screamed. It took me a long while to quiet her. Then I thought perhaps the scream had wakened Mother, and I came down to see."

He had not thought it possible for her pallor to increase until he saw her whiten—whiten until her color was that of the dusty plaster bust on the mantelpiece. He felt for the pulse in the wrist of the hand he held, but with a sudden motion she twisted loose from his grasp.

"Don't be professional with me. I'm all right. . . . Mother wasn't in her bed." She clasped her hands together on her knees and leaned forward. "I found her in the drawing room, in the big chair . . . I left her there—you saw—"

"Yes. You think she heard Lucy Anne scream and went to find her?"

"That must have been it."

"And she had just reached the chair when her heart stopped—that would be it, of course. She might not even have had time to call. And Lucy Anne?"

"She's still in my bed. I haven't wakened her. I was afraid to. What am I to tell her? The dream alone made her hysterical with fright."

"I'll tell her a little later. Just now I am going to make you some coffee and boil some eggs for us both, then you must go to bed and stay there. I can give you a bromide if you need it."

"Already I feel as if I had been drugged. I think I could rest thankfully forever and ever. But there are things to do."

"Your brothers to be notified. Write the telegrams, and Aaron can send them. I can send the undertaker, and your brother Tom should be here in time to see him."

"Lucy Anne?"

"Let me take her with me until after the funeral. It would be best for her."

"Oh, would you? How kind you are!"

"Kindness has become the wellspring of my being—since last night." He smiled at her briefly, and she noticed for the first time how drawn his face was. "What else can my life be built on? But don't think I could reproach you. . . . I'll tell Lucy Anne, after we've had some breakfast—then you must try to comfort her and persuade her to go with me. And you must go to bed."

"There is still the house to be opened up before the funeral. Mother can't be buried from the back door. . . ."

"This afternoon or tomorrow will be time enough for that. I'll have my old Dixie send her niece Roma to help you, and to do the cooking. She's a good darkie, and they all love funerals. . . . Besides, won't Tom's wife come over with him? . . . Now, tell me where you keep the coffee and the eggs, and while I am getting some breakfast for us, you lie down on the couch."

After the two of them had eaten, Dr. Martin went upstairs to Lucy Anne. Hilary washed the dishes, with the kitchen door closed, so that she could not hear their voices, upstairs. The night—she shivered—the night had made her cowardly. It was while she was in the library writing the telegrams to her brothers, that the doctor came down again, with Lucy Anne in his arms. He sat down with her in Hilary's chair beside the fire. She was still in her nightgown, but he had wrapped a blanket about her. Her black hair hung a tangled web about her face, which was tearstained and swollen.

"She has wept herself exhausted, Hilary—and she won't believe that she is to go home with me for a couple of days. Tell her—"

Hilary spoke quietly.

"Why not, Lucy Anne? You like Dr. Martin, and he hasn't anyone to look after him. It would be fun for him to have a little girl for a couple of days." She raised an eyebrow inquiringly at the doctor.

"Yes." He smiled at her above the child's head. "Just for these two days when your mother can spare you?"

"Oh, Mother! Can you—spare me?" There was a heartbroken appeal in the tear-choked voice.

"I shall be so busy, you see. There is so much to do. Besides, your Uncle Tom and Aunt Eleanore and Margaret will be here—"

"Oh!" She turned to the doctor. "Yes, I should like to go."

"That's a good girl. You can ride in my automobile with me. And old Dixie will give you whatever you want to eat, and help you to dress in the mornings and put you to bed—"

Lucy Anne suddenly remembered. "Oh, Mother! Oh, Mother!" she cried. "Do you suppose—Gran—do you suppose the—the *dream* killed her?"

Hilary rose from the table. Her face was set, stony in its withdrawal.

"No. Dreams are only dreams. Don't think of such a thing again." Her voice was cold and even. "Go now and get dressed. You mustn't keep Dr. Martin waiting. I'll be there in a minute to help you with your hair."

Without a word, and only a frightened glance at her mother, Lucy Anne slipped from the doctor's lap. She disappeared into the hall, trailing a corner of the blanket on the floor behind her. Hilary turned to Dr. Martin.

"You see," she said. "Don't let her dwell on what she dreamed. Please—" Urgency sharpened her voice. "Don't let her speak of it, even. . . . You have said yourself, often enough, the child is all too inclined to be morbid."

"Very well. I'll do my best."

Hilary gave him her hand in farewell.

"I shall not come down again. It is good of you to take her. There is no way I can even try to repay your kindness. I am sorry that things could not have been different."

She did not look sorry, nor glad. Her face was still like dusty plaster, lifeless and grayish white.

She gave Aaron all necessary instructions, and went upstairs to bed. There she lay all day in a kind of frozen indifference. She heard the colored woman in the kitchen, and at noon accepted the tray she brought her. She heard her brother Tom come in, with his family. Eleanore came to the door, but she pretended to be asleep.

When it was time for Will's train, the next day, she rose for the first time and dressed. She found that Eleanore had opened the house. The bedrooms had been aired and the beds made. Downstairs, all the covers had been taken from the furniture and put away. The shutters had been opened, and the rooms dusted. Her mother lay in her coffin in the drawing room, and the air was heavy with the scent of flowers. There was nothing for her to do; she went into the library and suffered Eleanore's tongue while she waited for Will.

When she heard his cab on the drive, her knees turned to water; she could not rise to meet him. He found her sunk in the deep chair beside the fire. He had not been told that she, too, had been ill. He concealed the shock he felt at sight of her: he said only "Hilary," and went to her with outstretched hands, and all the estrangement of the last years melted away into nothing.

"Hilary!" He kissed her. "No one told me that you were ill."

"I'm not—only tired to death. You will stand by me now, Will?"

"Of course." And he took her hot hands in his.

2

THE FUNERAL WAS OVER. HILARY AND HER TWO BROTHERS AND MRS. TOM BAIRD HAD RETURNED TO THE HOUSE. MRS. Baird's family had come over from the city for the funeral, and she had sent her daughter home with them. Margaret had wept noisily beside her grandmother's grave. Her mother had thought it very odd that Lucy Anne had not been there. "After your mother raised her like she was one of her own," she had complained in her husband's ear, in the undertaker's cab. "An' I reckon you'll find she's left her the property, too," she had added venomously. She had no intention of leaving the Baird house until she had heard the will read.

Now the four of them were in the drawing room, waiting for Mr. Robinson to come from his office with the will. A group of chairs had been drawn together in one of the bay windows. Mrs. Tom Baird sat in one of them, a wide rocking chair, her feet thrust far out in front of her, and her toes moved rhythmically back and forth as she rocked. Her husband had chosen the chair farthest from her, a stiff chair against the wall, and hoped that, since asides were impossible, she would hold her tongue.

Because the flower-scented room had seemed so close when they had come in, Hilary had gone to one of the front windows to open it; Will had followed her, and the two stood there, looking out across the terrace into the tangle of grass and maple trees that limited their view. The sun was shining, for the first time in days, and in its pale light the yellowed branches and the fallen leaves and the tawny grass were radiant and golden. The two were held there, their backs turned to the dark room behind them while they spoke in undertones that could not reach the others' ears.

"I suppose we have come to an end now of all this." Will spoke without regret.

" 'All this?' "

He nodded to indicate the scene before him.

"Mother's impossible dream."

"What dream?" Hilary spoke more sharply than she had intended.

"Mother's dream of establishing a kind of baronial family here, superior to everything and everybody. Of course it was impossible: too artificial in this kind of society. Life to be stable must be natural—"

Hilary laughed at him. "How men like to generalize . . . I have never thought of what Mother wanted, except as it affected us."

"But I am right, am I not? It was what she wanted. And no one can live alone among inferiors in a democratic society. One must either find one's equals, or sink to one's neighbors' level, or die of loneliness."

"You generalize, and leave me to say what you are thinking. You mean yourself and Tom and me . . . I suppose you are right."

"This place simply doesn't belong in this landscape. It is all wrong."

"Mother didn't think so."

"I know. Well—"

"We shall see."

Aaron led Mr. Robinson into the room, and they

turned to shake hands with him, and afterwards sat down side by side on the narrow green velvet Empire sofa that stood between the windows.

Hilary was not surprised to see that the lawyer fingered his briefcase with an air of embarrassment. He twirled his glasses on their ribbon, he fumbled with the straps of the case and extracted a paper which he could easily have carried in his pocket, he cleared his throat, coughed a little and cleared his throat again. Her mother's will, Hilary thought, would no doubt be an embarrassing document to have to read.

"This is a very trying moment for me." The lawyer finally found his voice. "For that reason I intend to get it done and over with as quickly as possible. That is why I have made no opening remarks not germane to the subject; I feel unequal to polite conversation with the ladies." He bowed in their direction. Hilary caught his eye and smiled. Under the most favorable conditions, polite conversation with her sister-in-law Eleanore was not to be undertaken lightly.

"I shall only say that I never felt that this—er—instrument was a just one, and I did all that I could to persuade your mother to change it."

Hilary felt Eleanore's eye upon her, speculative

and inimical, and knew that she was due for the most pleasant surprise of her life.

"Only a few weeks ago," Mr. Robinson resumed, "Mrs. Baird came into my office and added a codicil to the will which contradicts many of the provisions of the will itself. I therefore ask you not to exclaim at the will proper, but to let me read through the codicil."

He adjusted his glasses and cleared his throat again.

"I, Margaret Linley Baird, being of sound mind . . ." He waded through the legal phraseology of the introduction. . . .

"I direct that all my personal property, which today totals approximately three hundred thousand dollars, be divided in three equal portions. One portion is to be put in trust for my son William's children, the money to be divided among them equally and surrendered to them when the youngest reaches the age of twenty-one. I make this provision because my son William has all the money he needs for himself, and if he were given this in addition he would in all probability turn it over to my daughter Hilary.

"One portion is to be held in trust for my grand-daughter Lucy Anne, to be given to her when she arrives at the age of twenty-one, provided that she has been brought up in the family of her Uncle Thomas, and has received no musical education whatsoever.

"One portion is to be paid by my trustees to my son Thomas: twenty thousand dollars immediately following my death, if he consents, and is permitted by my daughter Hilary, to receive my granddaughter Lucy Anne into his family to be brought up as his own child; and thereafter twenty thousand dollars at intervals of three years, if she is still with him, and if he has seen to it that she has received no musical instruction of any kind; when my granddaughter Lucy Anne reaches the age of twenty-one he is to receive the balance of the portion due him, if there is any balance remaining, and if the above conditions have been kept.

"My real property . . ." and there followed an enumeration of the Baird lands, "is to be held intact for my granddaughter Lucy Anne, and is to be surrendered to her on her coming of age, to sell or to hold, as she pleases, on the condition that she opens up and consents to dwell in, and does dwell in, for at least ten years, ten months of each year, the house in which I now live, built by my father Thomas Linley. Until she comes of age, the income from the land is to be devoted to paying my granddaughter Lucy Anne's expenses, to the amount determined upon by my trustees. The income over and above such expenses is to be paid to my daughter Hilary annually, provided that she consents to allow my son Thomas to bring up her daughter Lucy Anne; if my daughter Hilary dies before her daughter Lucy Anne comes of age, this income is to be added to the funds in trust for the said Lucy Anne.

"If either my daughter Hilary or my son Thomas declines to accept the conditions here set down, all my personal property is to be put in trust for the children of my son William, to be divided among them when the youngest comes of age. If my granddaughter Lucy Anne at the age of twenty-one declines to live in the house aforesaid for ten years, ten months out of each year, the property is to be sold and the sums received divided among all my other grandchildren. If my son Thomas receives my granddaughter Lucy Anne into his family and keeps the stipulated conditions, but dies before the said Lucy Anne comes of age, the trustees shall appoint a guardian for her, and shall pay to my son's wife, or if she has died, to her daughter Margaret, whatever remains unpaid at the time of his decease of the third portion of my personal property bequeathed to him under the aforesaid conditions.

"If my granddaughter Lucy Anne should die before she reaches the age of twenty-one, her third portion of my personal property is to be paid to her mother, if she is still living, or to be divided equally among my other grandchildren, if she has died. If my granddaughter Lucy Anne dies before the settlement of the real property, it is to be sold and the moneys received divided among my other grandchildren.''

Out of the corner of his eye, Mr. Robinson could see Hilary, pale and composed, her lips shut in a thin line, and, in contrast, Mrs. Thomas Baird, flushed and swollen with indignation. Her lips were parted. . . . He hurried through the last paragraph of the will, which provided for the appointment of the trustees, and named him executor of the estate, and arranged for a bequest to Aaron. He read the signature of Mrs. Baird, the signatures of the witnesses, and paused to look up. Hilary's fingers were on her brother Will's arm.

"She thought I had not long to live," she murmured, "and besides, remember the codicil. Don't say anything. . . ."

The lawyer crackled the paper to attract their attention. They were once more silent, and Mrs. Thomas Baird gave up her attempt to speak.

"The codicil is dated September seventeenth. It is in your mother's own words, as she insisted upon having it.

"I have discovered that my granddaughter Lucy Anne would not be happy in my son Thomas's family. Therefore I direct that his third of my personal property be paid to him immediately following my death, unconditionally."

Eleanore stopped rocking, abruptly.

"Thank God for that," she exclaimed. "But she never give a thought to us—whether we'd be happy havin' the kid—"

Mr. Robinson quelled her with a glance.

"The third of my property which I have directed should be put in trust for Lucy Anne, to be paid under conditions, I still direct must be put in trust for her, to be paid to her on her twenty-first birthday provided that either of these different conditions are complied with:

"One. That my daughter Hilary marry Dr. Martin Child, and the two of them bring up my granddaughter Lucy Anne with no musical instruction whatsoever, and that in case such a marriage takes place and my daughter Hilary dies before her husband and before my granddaughter Lucy Anne comes of age, he, the said Dr. Martin Child, is made her guardian.

"Two. Or that, if my daughter Hilary does not marry Dr. Martin Child, she move at once to some climate where her tuberculosis can be cured or retarded, and that she keep Lucy Anne with her until Lucy Anne reaches the age of twenty-one, and she, the said Hilary, must not leave this country until that time, and must not allow her daughter Lucy Anne to have any musical instruction.

"If these conditions are kept, the income from the land is to be paid to my daughter Hilary yearly until her daughter Lucy Anne is twenty-one. If the conditions are not kept, she is to receive nothing, and my granddaughter Lucy Anne's third of my personal property is to be put in trust as aforesaid for my son William's children.

"If my daughter Hilary dies without marrying before my granddaughter Lucy Anne comes of age, I direct that my son William be made her guardian, and that he keep these same conditions: keep her in this country, and allow her no musical instruction, he to be paid the income from the land until she comes of age, to provide for her education."

Will Baird was on his feet before Mr. Robinson had finished reading the signatures attached to the codicil.

"It is fantastic—preposterous! She was mad, surely. It can't be valid, a will like that!"

Mr. Robinson shook his head.

"Fantastic, if you like. But she was not mad."

"On the contrary." Hilary spoke in a thin clear

voice, unshaken. "She has us all tied up neatly. When you think it over, Will, you will see just how clever she was."

"You can't accept it, Hilary, you can't. I told you she had cherished an impossible dream. She cared only to preserve this place—"

"No. Lucy Anne and the place together: more than anything in the world she wanted the child to belong here."

"But does she?"

Hilary shook her head.

"I thought not, or she wouldn't have hedged her about with such conditions. But you are not going to accept them? You know that if you refused, I should support you and Lucy Anne. I don't know what your hopes were, or your plans, but surely not this?"

"No. Other things are more important for Lucy Anne than her grandmother's money. But think what you are suggesting: if it cost you five thousand a year—and it wouldn't—to support us—it might count up, by the time Lucy Anne is of age, to sixty thousand dollars. That isn't half of her share of the property, which would go to your children."

"I see. You think my generosity would have a dubious look."

"Not to me. But your reputation—"

"I suppose you would not believe me, but my reputation is not so important to me as your happiness. . . . But I am certainly not in a situation to urge you to defy her wishes. What will you do?"

"I am too tired to care. . . . Take the child and go west . . . I may say that I am not going to marry Martin Child." She smiled a little.

"Has he asked you?" Insolent as she was, Eleanore dared only to mutter the question, but Hilary heard it.

"That is my affair—and his."

"H'mph! Mother Baird took a lot for granted, seems to me." She turned to Mr. Robinson. "Do I understand that Lucy Anne is to get all the land?"

"The codicil made no change in that provision of the will. Eventually, she will have the land, if she consents to live for ten years in this house. Otherwise, it is to be sold, and the money divided between the other grandchildren."

"Well, except for that," and she tossed her head, "except for that I call it a very sensible will. Codicil, I mean. If Hilary's got t.b. what else in the world could she do but try to get well?"

Hilary, who had turned her back, looked at her scornfully over her shoulder.

"You think that it matters to me whether I live

or die? It doesn't, not in the slightest. If I weren't so tired—"

She walked away from them, and went and stood in the window, looking out over the sunlit grass of the terrace. Mr. Robinson joined her.

"You agree to abide by the terms of the will, then?"

"What else is there to do?"

"I am sorry, Hilary. I did my best."

"I know. She complained of you." She smiled up at him. "How soon can we go?"

"At once, after the will is probated. This last year's income from the land will be yours."

After a moment's talk, they shook hands, and he picked up his briefcase and departed. Will went out too, to walk with him to the gate. Tom, in the drawing-room door, motioned to his wife to follow him to the library.

"Can't you see what she must be feeling?" he said. "Left without everything that should have been hers?"

Hilary when they had all gone, continued to stand in the window. Her only emotion was a sense of relief: it was all over—everything was over and done with. She had not been surprised at her mother's will: she had always known that the crisis in their struggle would come after her mother's death; she had been waiting for that crisis, husbanding her strength that she might face it . . . and she could not face it, after all. It was her acquiescence that surprised her, amused her, even. She could not reproach herself. Her mind was empty of everything: reproaches, intentions, memories—everything except the longing for peace. Perhaps it would have been different if she could have kept in her mind the reality of Paolo, but Paolo had left her . . . *she* could not even dream of him. . . .

Had she not said something to her mother once about "even to the edge of doom"? The question struck across the quiet of her thought.

She turned from the window and crossed the room slowly two or three times. There was no use in maudlin self-examination. She must find something to do, at once, this very instant. She could close up this part of the house again: latch the shutters, bolt the hall door, and put the slip covers back on the furniture—her brothers could sit in the library this evening.

She found the covers folded up and piled on a shelf in the cupboard in the hall; she carried them into the drawing room. On top lay the one that belonged on the chair in which her mother had died. When she shook it out, a crumpled piece of paper dropped to the floor.

"Something of Lucy Anne's," she thought, as she stopped to pick it up. "Something she left in the chair, and they missed seeing it when they took the covers off." Idly wondering, she unfolded it. It was covered with a minute, spidery writing: her mother's. She was surprised, but not startled, to see it; she turned and sat down in the chair to read.

But there was a date written across the top of the paper: October twentieth. When she saw that her hands were seized with trembling and she dropped them to her lap. It was the day her mother had died. She bent over the paper; the words, erratically penciled, swam before her eyes. She could barely decipher them:

"I, Margaret Linley Baird, being of sound mind on this night of October the twentieth in the year of Our Lord 19—, do hereby revoke the previous will made by me, and declare this to be my last will and testament. Let John Robinson, the executor of my estate, divide all my property, real and personal, equally and unconditionally, between my three children, William, Thomas, and Hilary."

Below, her name had been written once more, and under the name there ran another line of writing:

"I bequeath the rosewood piano to my granddaughter Lucy Anne."

Hilary relaxed in her chair to still her trembling. "It is too late," she thought, "I am too tired."

After a while she took up the paper again, to tear it into shreds. It threatened her peace.

But she was stopped by the question that she tried to keep from entering her mind.

"When had her mother written that paper?"

Of course it was not possible that it had been wrung from her by the power of Paolo's music, by Paolo, fighting for Lucy Anne after she had given up the fight. She did not believe that. But. . . .

If one-third of her mother's money was hers, unconditionally, what was there that she could not do? She was free. . . .

Paolo! And she had almost betrayed him again, by destroying the paper.

For a while she was too unstrung, too weak to move, but when she could rise she crossed the room to the rosewood piano; she opened it, and played on the untuned keys, very softly, the opening bars of the "Turkish March."

The door behind her opened. She turned and saw there her brother Will.

"I wondered where you had hidden yourself away," he said.

"Will! See what I found"—she held the paper out to him. "No, wait. I must explain. You understand that we found Mother dead in that chair there in the corner? And that the colored girl and Eleanore opened up this room for the funeral while I was in bed? They must have picked this paper up in the slip cover of that chair without seeing it, because I found it there. It was written by Mother the night she died. There was a lamp lighted in her bedroom when I came down: perhaps she felt herself dying and wrote it before she ever got out of bed."

He took the paper and read it.

"She came to her senses at the end. Poor Mother! But it was too late: you see, Hilary, there are no witnesses to the signature."

"Couldn't it be established if it were taken to court? It's so much fairer to everyone—and it means freedom to me, Will."

"I doubt it. The other will left our shares to our children: the court would hardly take it from them and give it to us."

Hilary thought swiftly.

"The income from the land. . . . In view of this will, don't you think the court might let me have that unconditionally? It is to be mine. . . . That would be enough. . . ."

"It is possible. I shall take this and consult Robinson. But at any rate, Hilary, I told you, I am perfectly willing to support you and Lucy Anne. The child's share of Mother's money would go to my children, then, but I could leave mine to her: it would all be the same in the end. I should have said this before, but you seemed so ready to accept Mother's conditions.''

"I was. But now I have girded my loins.'' She smiled at him, and sat down again at the piano.

"What is it that you plan?''

"You won't sympathize. But the child is a born musician.''

"You want her trained?''

Hilary nodded. "You will arrange things so we can go at once?''

"At once?'' He hesitated. "The child is so young—shouldn't you go west for a year or so first?''

"Surely you can see, Will,'' she spoke simply, directly, "there is very little time left me? I should take Lucy Anne and sail tomorrow if I could.''

"Hilary—'' But he knew there was no use in arguing with her. He took up the paper and went out.

There were tears in Hilary's eyes, but she did not follow him. She stayed at the piano, and played the Turkish March through to the end.

3

JUST BEFORE DINNER TIME, DR. MARTIN
BROUGHT LUCY ANNE TO THE HALL DOOR.
HILARY MET THEM AT THE THRESHOLD.

"Mother! I've come back."

"I am glad to have you back." Her mother smiled
at Dr. Martin over her head.

"Everything is all right?" he asked.

Hilary nodded. "Everything."

Lucy Anne came close to her mother.

"Then—I shan't have to live with Uncle Tom?"

"Oh, no! Your grandmother promised you that."

"I know. But—"

Hilary put her arm around Lucy Anne and held her tight to her side while she shook hands with Dr. Martin, and thanked him. Lucy Anne thought, "Grandmother is dead, and now she can love me a little," and she drew away from her mother and started up the back stairs. Hilary saw that she was crying, and followed after her and stood by the newel post.

"What is it, my dear child? Don't cry like that."

Lucy Anne shook her head and went on up the stairs. How could she tell her mother that she was crying because she could not be glad that she loved her now, because that would mean that she was glad that her grandmother was dead? Lucy Anne thought how she had never loved her grandmother enough; she remembered all the evenings they had sat on the porch to watch the sunset, when she had not wanted her grandmother to hold her hand. She went on up the stairs without looking back, and in her own room, on her own bed, she wept into her pillow because she had never given her grandmother what she had wanted, and now her grandmother was dead.

It was not until dinner was ready that Hilary went up to Lucy Anne's room and sat beside her on the bed.

"It's dinner time. But first I wanted to tell you: your grandmother left you the piano."

"The *rosewood piano?*"

"Yes."

"Then—then, Mother—was it a dream?"

"Of course it was a dream. The piano was a present from your grandmother that was meant to say that she knew she had been mistaken."

"Then you think she wouldn't mind now if I were to be a musician?"

"No, she wouldn't mind now."

Lucy Anne caught her breath.

"How soon, Mother? How soon?"

"As soon as we can get to Italy."

"Italy!"

As they reached the foot of the stairs, Will Baird came in the door.

"This is your Uncle Will, Lucy Anne." Hilary put both hands on the child's shoulders and turned her toward him. He kissed her, and then they went into the dining room where the others were waiting.

"Robinson thinks the court will give Hilary the income from the land and release her from the conditions imposed by Mother. But you mustn't wait for it to be settled, Hilary. I'll see that you have all that you need."

They sat down, and the meal began, but they were not at ease. Tom particularly, was uncomfortable and unhappy.

"I'll divide my share of the estate with you, Hilary. She didn't make provision for any such contingency." He smiled grimly. "Hardly expected me to be so generous, I suppose." He dared not look at his wife. "But I'll not get it soon enough to do you any good. You should go west tomorrow."

"I shall not need your money, Tom. The income from the land is all I'll want. Besides—"

"You are going west, aren't you?"

They all looked at her and waited. She shook her head. She knew that when she spoke she would bring the house in tumult about her ears.

"Where, then?"

"Italy."

"Italy!" Their exclamations were a bombardment in her ears; it was as if the word had released them suddenly from all restraint, so that they could say all the things that ought not to be said.

"Why Italy?"

"It would be suicidal. You would never get there."

And again, "Why?"

Her eyes met Lucy Anne's; they both smiled. They knew why.

"To put Lucy Anne in the school in Milan—where you put me some twenty years ago, Will, remember? There she will have the education she is entitled to—the best training in music in the world."

Eleanore answered her, and her words were an echo of her mother-in-law.

"I should think you'd had enough of musicians to last a lifetime."

Hilary only looked at her coldly, but Will spoke in her defense.

"Paolo was the greatest violinist there was, for a while, there's no doubt about that, and if Lucy Anne inherits his genius. . . . He wasn't a bad fellow in many ways. But," and his voice quickened, spurred by dislike; he forgot his original motive for speaking. "He was a scoundrel with women, and those concerts in New York ruined him. New York went to his head. Why didn't you divorce him, Hilary? It would have saved your life. . . . Forgive me—I've never asked you that before, and have no business to now . . . I spoke without thinking."

But Eleanore would not spare her.

"If she hadn't been weak-kneed, she would have. Why didn't you, Hilary?"

"I am not sure that I owe anyone an explanation, but I had several reasons, and I am not ashamed of any of them." Hilary spoke quietly, but she had put down her knife and fork, and had taken hold of the edge of the table. "In the first place, he was a Catholic."

"But you weren't."

"No. But he had that idea: that we were married for eternity, and I thought, why not encourage him in it?" Hilary laughed oddly. "In the second place, if I had, he might have had to marry—another woman—and he would have been unhappy, and would have hated me if I had let him in for that."

"Seems to me I wouldn't have cared. It would have served him right."

Hilary's voice when she answered was very soft, her manner almost mocking, but there was a dangerous light in her eyes.

"Ah, but I haven't told you my third reason—my real reason. I suppose you do not understand what the word means, but I loved him."

"Then you were as bad as he was. How any right-minded woman could love a low-down skunk—"

Hilary sprang up. Her silverware clinked together on the table, her chair scraped across the floor. By her rigidity they saw that it was only by the utmost endeavor that she kept her self-control.

"You forget, Eleanore, that you are speaking of the father of my child in her presence. Come away, Lucy Anne . . . I shall expect not to have to see you again while you are here."

She went out the door, and the bewildered and indignant child rose to follow her. No one spoke until Lucy Anne turned, on the threshold. They saw her clench her fists in the folds of her skirt.

"I'll tell you why she would not stop loving him. It was because if she had—if she had, he would have been undone, and *they would never meet on that peaceful shore to sing the song of Zion forever!*" She flung the words at them, turned on her heel, and slammed the door behind her.

4

IN ANOTHER DAY LUCY ANNE AND HER MOTHER WERE LEFT ALONE AGAIN, WITH NOTHING TO DO BUT WAIT UNTIL THE TIME should come for them, too, to go. When the child felt the desolation of the old house closing in about her, she wished that they could have gone with her Uncle Will: wished that they had made an end to everything before they had had time to think about how it was to end.

Hilary would take nothing with them except the clothes they would need on the way to New York. Sorrowfully, Lucy Anne piled her books away in the drawers below the bookcases; she glanced inside the cover of each one for the last time before she put it in; when they were put away and the drawers closed, she looked up at her mother with a kind of horror in her face.

"Mother—when we're gone, this part of the house will be just like the other part. Dust will come in here, too—"

"Yes. Dust and cobwebs." There was no suggestion of regret in Hilary's voice.

"But of course as long as Aaron is here, to remember, we'll be here, too." Aaron was to stay on the place as caretaker, under the supervision of Mr. Robinson. "We'll be *there* really, but for Aaron we'll be here. How queer: to be in two places at once. And we'll never know what we may be doing in Aaron's mind. And Grandmother—Grandmother will be here, too, for Aaron. But she won't be anywhere else at the same time. And when Aaron is dead, she won't be anywhere at all. . . ." Lucy Anne had spoken half under her breath, staring out the window, but now she turned toward her mother. "Grandmother will never be with us, because she can't be where she never was. Can she?"

"Lucy Anne, do go outside and play in the sunshine for an hour."

The child left the room, but she did not go outdoors. Instead, she opened the door into the drawing room. She felt that the time had come for her to make her farewell tour of the house.

The room looked as it had looked ever since she had first seen it. The chairs were shrouded in white covers, the chandeliers tied up in bags. The shutters were closed, and it was dark as night, the darkness only accentuated by a stray glimmer of light reflected from one of the dim gold-framed mirrors. It looked the same, but to Lucy Anne there was a difference. There was nothing at all in the room now: nothing but four silent walls and a few old pieces of furniture. There was no more echoes of voices or footsteps or laughter, there were no echoes at all. There was no one left to remember voices and footsteps, that was why. She thought how much the death of any one person took out of the world: it took all that that person had remembered.

For a moment Lucy Anne stood stark still beside the piano—her piano—conscious only of the black emptiness of the room, and then she turned and went back to the hall door.

"Oh, Mother! Come play for me on the piano— just once—will you, please?"

"Why?" Her mother came into the hall.

"Because. Because—I should like to know again for sure that nothing else matters—"

Hilary laughed as she opened the piano and dusted the keys with her handkerchief.

"Open the shutters. . . . What shall I play?"

"Play what I dreamed that night."

Lucy Anne listened, and her throat tightened with emotion, her heart lifted with exultation. There was nothing in the world but this: nor walls nor rooms nor house. "Thy walls shall shake at the noise of the horsemen, when he shall enter into thy gates." It was terrible. "Terrible like an army with banners." And then she remembered, in some confusion of mind, that it was love which was terrible. "Thou art beautiful, my love . . . terrible like an army. . . ." She grasped at the understanding which was almost hers, so long as the music played. Remember whom you love, and so long as you remember, he can never die. Of course it was terrible, love like that.

When Hilary came to an end, the child was staring at her, wide-eyed.

"Mother," she said softly, wondering at her own boldness, "were you ever sorry that you loved my father?"

"Sorry? No. It was that that held my life together. Like the motif of a piece of music." She sounded a triumphant chord on the piano. "Love was the only thing in my life that gave it a reason for being." She spoke lightly, but she had turned the piano stool halfway round, and sat looking out the window, outside where all the leaves had fallen from the maple trees, and you could see between their branches for a long way, even to the distant iron fence. Lucy Anne knew that her mother was not thinking of her. And she knew now that if her mother had never thought of her, it was because of Paolo—Paolo who had never died.

HELEN HOOVEN SANTMYER: A Profile

XENIA OHIO—WITH THE EXCEPTION OF THE TORNADO TEN YEARS AGO, THE MOST NEWSWORTHY EVENT IN XENIA in this century has been the announcement that *". . . And Ladies of the Club"* by eighty-eight-year-old Xenian Helen Hooven Santmyer was to be reissued by G. P. Putnam's Sons and has been chosen as the August Book-of-the-Month selection.

As soon as it was announced, the media arrived at Hospitality House East, where the author has lived since 1982, with cameras, microphones, tape recorders, and notebooks to fire questions at the writer. As many as forty reporters crowded the reception area of the home in one day.

". . . And Ladies of the Club" follows the lives of members of a women's literary club in Waynesboro (read Xenia) from 1863 to 1932. Their lives—marriages, children, grandchildren, deaths—and those of scores of other members over the years, are de-

tailed against the political, religious, medical, legal, and industrial history of those seventy-five years.

"What a prodigious amount of research you did," young interviewers say to the author. "Not at all," she answers. "Except for checking the dates and a few small details, it was all in my life's experience. I wrote what I knew."

Xenia city fathers have commissioned a plaque to be mounted on the Santmyer family home at 133 West Third Street.

Brown-eyed, gray-haired Helen Santmyer is taking the fuss with good grace. She thinks all the bustle is fun, although she is disconcerted because the young reporters want instant information. She likes to take time to consider her responses, but modern media do not stay for the answers.

She has frailties—heart trouble, some arthritis and emphysema—but her lifelong interests in reading, sports, politics, games, and conversation have not diminished.

Helen, born in Cincinnati in 1895, went to Xenia with her parents, Joseph and Bertha Hooven Santmyer, when she was three. She has a younger sister, Jane Anderson, who lives in Xenia, and a brother, Philip, of Houston. Her father was associated with the Kelly Company, makers of rope and twine.

Her first memory of the town is of the courthouse

on a summer afternoon, with the hot sun drenching the tiled roof and wilting the elm trees that surrounded the building. The four-sided clock in the courthouse tower has always been an essential part of Xenia lives.

When Helen was growing up, the clock was lighted only until midnight. "There was a queer mixture of impressions on the mind," she wrote in *Ohio Town,* her third book, "when out of doors late at night, a first glance toward it showed the courthouse tower wiped out and a black hollow in the sky in its stead: Blank surprise followed by the scuttling, frightened whisper down old paths in the brain: 'It's late—awfully late,' and then by a sense of exhilaration at one's audacity—all in an instant, before maturity could assert itself against those echoes."

Midnight was the ultimate hour when Xenia girls and boys had to be in after a party. Once, at a farmhouse party, the clock struck midnight and the party broke up in a panic. When their horse clattered into town, Helen and her beau saw with relief and chagrin that the clock was still lighted. The farmer's clock was on sun time; they could have stayed a half hour longer.

In early days, Helen's grandmother attended the Methodist-supported Female Seminary on Church Street, as did two aunts. "When I was a child,"

Helen says, "they never impressed me as being learned or intellectual." More representative of the seminary was that group of elderly ladies who were distinctly, in an elegant, white-glove way, Blue Stockings, and who, through the Women's Club, the D.A.R., and the library board, spoke as the town's authorities in all matters literary, artistic, and historical.

"During my childhood, when the Women's Club assembled at a house in the neighborhood, you suspended your rowdy games while carriages stopped at the curb; you watched in awe until they were all indoors; and then you withdrew to a remote back yard lest the rude breath of another world disturb the delicate air they breathed."

It was twelve of these women from the Female Seminary who formed the club in *". . . And Ladies of the Club."*

Helen attended the Xenia public schools for twelve years, along with some forty other boys and girls. She was mischievous, yet intelligent. Although she loved school, she never really liked her teachers. In fact, one she hated. Her first-grade teacher, Miss Baker, shook her so hard one day that she bit her tongue. Helen had refused to stand up straight on command. She never forgave her teacher.

Early in her school years, Helen decided to be a writer. The decision came after she read *Little Women*. Years later she wrote of Derrick, the heroine in her first novel, *Herbs and Apples*:

> *Derrick sat alone on the terrace steps and stared with unseeing eyes across the dusky lawn at trees and fountain. Her heart thumped in her breast, in her ears, and she breathed heavily; the world rocked beneath her. A revelation had come to her from the last pages of the book she had been reading:* The Life, Letters and Journals of Louisa May Alcott. *The veil had been lifted, she had Known. She would be a Great Writer when she grew up.*

The church played an important part in growing up in Xenia. Helen attended the church of her great-grandparents, her grandmother, and her mother, the Presbyterian church on Market Street. "Searching back in my memory," she says, "I find no beginning of my knowledge of that vast auditorium, bare and clean in a cool clarity of light, its amplitude of air shaken by the music of the organ when all the stops were pulled for the doxology."

Dressed in her Sunday clothes and carrying her Bible and quarterly under her arm, Helen walked to Sunday school with her sister and brother. They rehearsed their catechism as they passed through the alley, across Second Street and Main Street, past houses of family friends.

They thought they understood what the Calvinist doctrine meant and considered it superior to that of the Methodists. Many were the school recess-time arguments between the Presbyterians and the Methodists, with the Episcopalians, the German Reformed, and the Baptists listening on the sidelines.

During Helen's high school days, the town held a revival in a tabernacle built for the occasion. Helen attended on Friday nights and was surprised to learn that in the eyes of the Lord, all denominations were equal.

After the revival, the town's young people attended Sunday-evening services at churches other than their own. As a high school girl, Helen disapproved of the Episcopalians, who read their prayers and rattled them off in an unintelligible singsong: she did not like their tiresome bobbing up and down, on and off their knees.

She thought the Methodist hymns were loud and noisy, and the United Presbyterians ungracious because while the Presbyterians sang the psalms in the UP church, the UPs stood mute during the Presbyterian hymns.

High school studies in Xenia were rigid. Everybody took at least three years of math, two of science, four of English, and four of Latin. She often looked out of the school library windows, toward fields and pastures beyond the town. "You looked and longed to be out and away," she said, "whether just to cross those fields to the nearest woods where violets and wild phlox grew or whether to cross the horizon and never come back."

She did cross the horizon in 1914, to spend four years at Wellesley College. Helen graduated from Wellesley in 1918. Her plans were to do graduate work at Oxford University, but her father said that she would have to stay home a year before he would send her abroad to study. As a result, she lived at home for a year and taught English in Xenia High School. She also began writing a novel.

The next year she secured a secretarial position with Charles Scribner's Sons in New York and shared an apartment on Eighty-second Street with a friend she met in New York. She completed the novel *Herbs and Apples* during the New York years.

It is autobiographical. The book is written in the first person, but the storyteller is a minor character. The heroine, Derrick, is in many respects Helen Santmyer.

She put into Derrick's mind her own beliefs that

"a woman's life is governed by her desire to win someone's approval—not just a lover's or a husband's, necessarily, but the person she cares most about. Perhaps the approval of a group of persons—but only in rare cases of the multitude."

When *Herbs and Apples* was accepted for publication by Houghton Mifflin, Helen left for England and graduate study at Oxford. She was twenty-eight.

She enrolled as a home student, as did all American women students at the time. She lived in the town. Her tutor was a Rhodes scholar—very pleasant but not much of a tutor. She pursued her studies independently and chose as her thesis subject a kindred soul, an eighteenth-century novelist, Clara Reeve (1729–1807), who wrote three Gothic novels and two based on English life in her own day. Her thesis was accepted and Helen received a degree in literature in 1927.

Herbs and Apples had been published while she was at Oxford. On her return to Xenia, Helen obtained, with the help of her friend, Mildred Sandoe, a position with the Dayton and Montgomery County Public Library. She lived at home and commuted. In her off hours she wrote a second novel, *The Fierce Dispute,* which was published in 1929. It foreshadows *". . . And Ladies of the Club"* in that it is a story of a small-town girl growing up in a home that had been occupied for years by her ancestors.

Neither of Helen's books was a best-seller. Because she was not a professional librarian, her work at the library was a dead-end job. In 1953, she became head of the English department and dean of women at Cedarville College. She continued to write during her teaching years, setting down in longhand stories from her childhood and descriptions of the Xenia where she grew up. In 1956, a nostalgic essay, "The Cemetery," appeared in the *Antioch Review.* It gave an account of childhood Sunday-afternoon walks in the town burying ground. "We used to follow haphazardly the twists in the road as they opened out," she wrote. "We might pause to note some new clayey mound or cross the grass to see who had lain so long in the earth that the name of his headstone had filled with lichens or even, holding our breaths, to peek through the broken corner of a moss-grown sarcophagus."

Even more interesting than the gravestones were the cemetery records that gave the names of the dead, the date of death, the next of kin, the cause of death, the name of the undertaker, and the location of the grave. "Historians and novelists may turn to the records when they please," she wrote, "and recreate with its help the town of a hundred or eight-five or seventy years ago."

As she wrote, she planned two books, a profile of her home town and a novel about the families whose members lay in the cemetery.

Cedarville College was a United Presbyterian school, founded in 1887. In 1928, when the sponsoring church affiliated with the Presbyterian Church of the U.S.A., the college became independent, giving four-year courses leading to the B.A. and B.S. degrees in education.

In March of 1953 came the announcement that Cedarville would merge with the Baptist Bible College of Cleveland, with the 100-student Baptist school moving to the Cedarville Campus. The General Associations of the Regular Baptists would operate the school.

The new administrator, Dr. James T. Jeremiah, called the faculty together and asked them to sign a statement that each believed every word in the King James version of the Bible as it was printed and would promise never to smoke, drink, or dance.

Helen could not in honesty sign the statement, but even if she could have, she would have refused on philosophical grounds. She resigned. In the end, Jeremiah fired the entire Cedarville faculty.

Helen returned to her job at the Dayton library, until her retirement in 1960. The following year, her profile of Xenia, *Ohio Town,* was published by the Ohio State University Press.

She continued to live in the big house on Third Street after the death of her father and mother. She began her novel, writing in large ledger books.

Mildred Sandoe, who had taken a job in the Cincinnati Public Library as director of personnel, drove back and forth daily from Xenia. Because the trip made her very late every day, Helen said, "Why don't you stop here on your way home, and I'll have your dinner ready."

After a while, Mildred sold her house and moved in permanently with Helen.

Mildred helped Helen every bit of the way through *". . . And Ladies of the Club."* Weldon Kefauver, editor of the Ohio State University Press, asked for the book as soon as he knew Helen was working on it. After about sixteen years, the manuscript was delivered.

It was much too long. Kefauver asked Helen to cut out seven hundred fifty pages. It was during the editing that Mildred worked hardest. "I would read her a passage and say, 'This could come out.' Helen would say, 'Well, put a check mark in the margin.'

The next day she would tell me whether to take it out or leave it in."

"I didn't want to cut any of it," says Helen. "I thought if people wanted to, they could skip part of it."

Late in 1983, Gerald Sindell, a California film producer, visited his mother in Shaker Heights. She had recently read an old library copy of *". . . And Ladies of the Club"* and told her son it was the best book she had ever read. He read it and saw it might be a bonanza for his business. The result of his promotion efforts was that Putnam decided to reprint the book, the Book-of-the-Month Club picked it up, and talk of TV and film rights proliferated.

The first flurry of interviews and callers had died down, but Helen Hooven Santmyer knows that it is not all over.

The preceding biographical sketch was excerpted from a feature story by Roz Young, which appeared in *The Magazine* of the Dayton (Ohio) *Daily News* on July 1, 1984, shortly before the reissuing of *". . . And Ladies of the Club."*